JYESTHA DEVI

Jyestha Devi
by Aboli Mane
Paperback Edition

First Published in 2024 in India by

Inkfeathers Publishing
Vivek Vihar, New Delhi 110095
www.inkfeathers.com

Content Curation Partner

ISBN 978-81-19483-66-2

JYESTHA DEVI

The Goddess of Misfortune

ABOLI MANE

INKFEATHERS PUBLISHING
www.inkfeathers.com

CONTENT CURATION PARTNER

To the daughters; to those were wronged
To the ambitious women; to women who yearned for love
but settled for compromise; to every woman who essayed a role
or has been called '*misfortune*', this book is for you.

***

To my parents who never gave up on me.
This book is a debt that I can never repay.

***

To my siblings, friends, and my mentors,
I owe you everything for your belief in my capabilities.

Contents

Preface

I know that most readers skip this part. I do it as well. I am far too excited to get into the story and open the doorways to a new adventure. Reading a book is a journey and the preface is a pit stop that few choose to make. However, some of you may have the question, "Who is Jyestha Devi? Why did you choose to write her story?"

Simply put, I had three different ideas in mind, but it was my mother's suggestion that led to the conception of this novel. "Why don't you write a story on Alakshmi?" Alakshmi or Jyestha is a little-known character in Hindu mythology. I grew up reading the tales from the *Ramayana* and *Mahabharata*, and this interest turned into a quest for knowledge which led me to reading the *Puranas*.

The story of Alakshmi appears in the *Uttara Khanda of the Padma Purana* where she is born before Lakshmi from the churning of the ocean. Alakshmi or Jyestha is also mentioned in *the Linga Purana, the Vishnu Purana* and *the Skanda Purana* where she is driven away during the night of Deepavali before the worship of Lakshmi. Alakshmi is also mentioned briefly in *Atharva-Veda* where a hundred types of Lakshmi's follow a person after their birth, divided into the auspicious and inauspicious kind.

Alakshmi is often called *kalahapriya*, the one who is fond of discord and is the deity of inauspiciousness and ill-luck, married to Rishi Dussaha (Uddalaka or Kapila). Other *puranas* mention her as the wife of the Gandharva Kali or of Mrityu the god of decay or even Shanischara (Saturn). The worship of Jyestha Devi was once popular, but the deity then faded into obscurity. Some icons of Jyestha are found in the Kailasantha temple in Kanchipuram. She is depicted seated on a throne with a blue lotus in one hand, a water pot and a broom, flanked by two attendants (or children).

Alakshmi is everything that Lakshmi is not, and it is the duality between the two sisters that forms the crux of my novel. The Jyestha in my novel might stray from the depictions in the classical texts, as might her husband the Gandharva Kali, however that is my creative license as a fiction writer. While this novel is a work of fiction, it does not aim to offend any sentiments and should not be taken as an academic work. It is a family drama and the evolution of the goddess of misfortune Jyestha who faces every adversity and rises from her station as a little-known deity.

Why is Jyestha the goddess of adversity? And how do we overcome our personal adversities and find our identity? My debut novel pays homage to all the women that have suffered innumerable adversities, those that have been name-called or disrespected because their choices did not align with the expectations of those around them. It is a homage to the Jyestha within everyone.

1.

Emergence from Poison

Jyestha emerged in the midst of death and chaos. The flames of the enraged Vasuki sent a plume of smoke and fire that charred the Asuras near his mouth. The poison that dripped from the celestial Naga darkened the purity of the *Kshirsagar*. Halahala, the deadly poison spread its dark veins blackening the ocean of milk and from it, Jyestha assumed her dreadful shape, shimmering like a dark flame. Her footsteps left a sooty trail on the ivory sand. The cooling milky waves curdled under her soles.

Jyestha's coppery eyes gleamed in the divine light of Vaikuntha. The sky was a brilliant blue. Clear and untouched. It was too bright. Its splendor was charming.

What would it be like to rule this realm? Jyestha wondered.

A light wind rose as her eyes scanned the gritty shores. In the distance, a gathering buzzed like a beehive. Jyestha noted the uncertainty among the gathering. Her curly hair fluttered unbound. Her gait was unsteady. She fiddled with the drape of the blood-red *uttariya*, which shielded her dusky, corpulent form. She was the merit of the labour of the celestials on the eleventh day of the churning of the ocean.

Why does the gathering appear so cold?

A light wind sang across the tension that thickened like poison within this gathering, laden with a subtle scent. Jyestha upturned her face toward that fragrance. Her prominent nose quivered. The scent triggered a longing within her. Where were the sounds of the drums? Why was no one coming forward to welcome her? The Deva and the Asura camp stretched on either side of the great Naga Vasuki, who still writhed, yoked as the churning rope.

Apprehensively, Jyestha glanced at the gigantic, hooded serpent. His poison birthed her. This meant he was her father. Why did he not claim her? She walked to the midst of the gathering, head held with pride. Everyone was watching. The faces of Devas, Asuras, Gandharvas and other divine beings blurred and shifted. The emotion reflected within those faces mirrored like a reflection on a still water. Fear and contempt. The whispers thickening within either side churned a sea of fear in her heart.

She stood on the glimmering sands, her coppery eyes wide as the celestial gathering assessed her fate. The omens were unfavorable. Jyestha's heartbeat like a drum.

Born from poison, you are Alakshmi. O goddess, you are the harbinger of misfortune. O, elder sister of Lakshmi, you shall create chaos wherever you go.

The words of the Creator Brahma resounded upon Jyestha's ears like a thunderbolt. As her eyes darted from Devas to Asuras, they all stepped back. Their faces were wrought with tension. No celestial was brave enough to accept misfortune.

No one wanted her.

The realisation left her seething. How dare they insult her! Jyestha glared from the Deva Indra to the Asura Virochana, then to the *apasaras* and *gandharvas*. Their coronets sparkled in the divine light and their jewels flashed. Nobody spoke. Nobody moved. The eyes of the gathering were averted, and their heads were bowed.

At that critical moment, as Jyestha waited for acknowledgement the sound of the celestial drums diverted everyone's attention. Golden-hued nectar oozed from the heart of the churning as the Mount Mandara spun. From it, her twin arose, shining with the effulgence of a golden sun. Lakshmi, the goddess of fortune and luck. Her footsteps glimmered like gold. The currents parted to make a path for her. The Devas and Asuras, stirred rushing to fawn over Lakshmi, leaving Jyestha stranded on the shore.

Jyestha's mouth dropped open in shock. She blinked in confusion as a knot tightened in her belly.

I'm being ignored? But why? Am I not a goddess as well? A Devi?

In front of Jyestha's bewildered stare, Lord Vishnu, the Protector of the cosmos claimed the hand of her sister Lakshmi. The celestials rejoiced. Their happiness smarted like an open wound. Jyestha clenched her fists, seething even more with rage.

It's unfair! The elder sister has the first right to choose her Lord!

Lakshmi smiled benevolently. The shy smile that flitted across Lakshmi's face and the tender way the Lord gazed at his would-be bride made Jyestha's heart lurch. Tears prickled her eyes. That smile scorched like an insult within which was already turning virulent with envy and humiliation within her mind. It amplified when Lord Varuna claimed Lakshmi as his daughter in the presence of all, while Jyestha's father Vasuki ignored her.

Why are our fortunes so divisive?

Why am I the goddess of misfortune?

Why does neither side want me?

The sympathy within Lakshmi's gaze fanned the rage that burned within Jyestha's heart.

"Although, the Lord has accepted me as his wife, I must put forth the matter that my elder sister Jyestha is yet unwed." Lakshmi's soft voice made Jyestha scoff. Why was her sister feigning sympathy? The gathering shifted uncomfortably. The deafening roar of the sea waves was the only answer.

The air in Vaikuntha was pure, however it made Jyestha's stomach roil. Lord Shiva and Goddess Parvati watched from the top of Mount Mandara, Jyestha's eyes scanned the divine consorts. Beseechingly. However, the divine couple bestowed a benevolent smile, without interference.

What is that supposed to mean? If I am a goddess, the right match for me must be a god. However...

"I will marry her." Jyestha raised her head. Among the gathering, there was a group of sages. Jyestha had ignored the group, choosing to focus on the Devas or Asuras instead. The ones that might match her status as a goddess. A thin line of worry creased between her eyebrows. Who was that?

The speaker singled himself out from the gathering, standing between Jyestha and the group of the celestials. A tall gaunt *rishi*. His dark body was lean and sinewy due to eons of penance. A long silver beard graced his stern visage. Matted silver hair were coiled on top of his head. He wore a pure white *angavastra*, the ends of which were sodden by the waters of the Kshirsagar. A thin sacred thread shone in a silver gleam draped crossways about his torso. The sage's gaze was calm and penetrating, as though he could read the minutest thoughts within her. Jyestha nearly stumbled backward.

This...old man? Why is no one protesting?

Jyestha's coppery gaze was tinged with worry. An icy feeling clenched her heart as though it was being squeezed. Words failed her, she did not dare utter a word although the contempt that swirled within her was as furious as the churning that had birthed her. A cold trickle of sweat dripped down her jaw. She hoped someone would speak out against the logical fallacy of an old sage marrying a young woman especially when Jyestha was unwilling to accept him as a bridegroom.

If Lakshmi's hand can be claimed by Deva that matches her status, then why not mine?

Yet the fear of offending the sage constricted her throat. Jyestha had the foreknowledge that a *rishi's* curse could bring about destruction. The Devas and the Asura's had to churn the Kshirsagar, because Sage Durvasa had cursed Lord Indra that he would be divested of his fortune. Jyestha was afraid that if she spoke, it would invite unnecessary destruction. She turned her eyes to the Trimurti again, Brahma, Vishnu and Shiva, to assess if anyone would object.

"Are you sure, Sage Dussaha?" Narada Muni, the emissary of Lord Vishnu asked the sage. No one asked for Jyestha's opinion. She stood there, reeling from the implications of their silence. Jyestha could not help but glare at her sister Lakshmi, as though everything was her fault.

Dussaha? Even I'm clever enough to know his name means intolerable. I will never love him.

Lakshmi avoided her eyes. That was it. This was all her fault. The dissatisfaction that had been festering within her bubbled like Halahal. Her gaze darted to the Naga Vasuki. Her father had resumed his humanoid form and his silver eyes gleamed in a detached manner. Jyestha adjusted her garments again, fidgeting restlessly. Her head was still high as she advanced to seek her father's blessings. Whispers rushed around her, as the Naga King and his son-in-law exchanged greetings.

Vasuki placed the auspicious red veil on her face. Jyestha didn't have a moment to glimpse Sage Dussaha's expression. The red veil obscured her eyes and her skin prickled as Dussaha's gnarled hand clasped hers when the celestials' uttered benedictions. Unbroken rice grains rained from above upon the married couple.

"By the vow of *Prajapatya vivah,* I, your father unites you and Rishi Dussaha in matrimony. May you both perform your duties well."

For a moment, Jyestha's inner tribulations receded. There was that lingering scent again. An unknown fragrance that beckoned her. Jyestha wanted to raise her head and chase after it. To run away. *Towards what?* She asked herself. Her husband's grip on her hand was firm. The texture of his hand did not promise a life filled with delicacy or comfort. Through the monotony of the ritual before the sacred fire erected by Sage Dussaha, Jyestha glimpsed the hands of several Devas and Asuras. Her gaze strayed towards Lakshmi's clasped hands. Jyestha upturned her own right palm which hung loosely.

Is this all that's written in my fate? To be the wife of a sage, unadorned and toiling? Persevering endlessly to gain spiritual powers in for the glory of my Lord?

Jyestha thought about the tales she knew. As an ayonija (not born from a womb) she possessed the foreknowledge as did those that emerged with her. Jyestha didn't have to learn about the history of the cosmos before she was born. She was already aware of it as though it existed within her. The tales of Anasuya and Arundhati, two daughters of Rishi Kardama. Their glories did not belong to them alone. They were an adornment of their husband's fame. Anasuya's chastity which humbled the Trimurti, so that they were born as babies to great lady. Arundhati's form could not be replicated by Devi Svaha to please her Lord Agnideva, such was her purity. There was also the tale of Diti and Aditi, daughters of Daksha Prajapati and the mothers of the Asuras and Devas who vied for power over the dominion of their sons.

The one that hit closer was the tale of enmity between Garuda, the king of birds and Lord Vishnu's divine steed and the Nagas who thirsted for amrita. Kadru and Vinita were sisters, yet their relations were spoiled due to Kadru's enslavement of the latter. Jyestha wondered how Vasuki coped with it. The divine Naga's temperament was equivalent to that of a sage, he appeared detached from the grudges that were attributed to the Nagas. He lived like a hermit.

Jyestha and Dussaha bowed before Vasuki, seeking his blessings. As Jyestha touched her adoptive father's feet, an unsolicited wish stirred in her heart.

I wish I had a mother.

Startled by her own superficial desire, Jyestha pressed the veil to her eyes. Why was her heart brimming? As an *ayonija*, she was special. As was her sister Lakshmi. She felt the soft paternal touch on the crown of her head, but it offered her little comfort. It wasn't what the poison within her heart sought. Her sister's perfumed embrace was cloying at best. Lakshmi slipped gold and green bangles onto her wrists, graced her neck with pearls. Jyestha did not have a significant dower, yet her sister was doing her bit. Vasuki placed a single necklace of gems, sourced from the ocean around her neck.

She is the one with the better fortune.

Jyestha clenched her fist, pressed her lips into a smile and bowed before the gathering, her neck garlanded, her vision obscured and the hand of the old rishi gripping her left palm. It was always the sister pairs that brought fame, be it to their sons or their husbands, to their fathers or their brothers. Lakshmi would be worshiped. Alakshmi would be scorned. When Prajapati Brahma spoke those words that decided her fate, Jyestha's heart refused to accept it.

So be it then. Tathastu.

Jyestha's identity was erased like her sooty footprints on the silvery sand. She turned her back to Vaikuntha's opulence, on the scintillating crystal palaces, on the gold domed cupolas shimmering with encrusted jewels and her dream of being a reigning Queen. The soothing roar of the Kshirsagar that birthed her seemed to beckon her back like a weeping mother. However, Jyestha walked on, yoked to her husband like a cow to its master. Her slender neck remained unbent and though her gaze was obscured, her coppery eyes smelted like a furnace.

I will return. When I do, the celestials will rue this day of my insult.

Jyestha vowed. She became Alakshmi, the harbinger of misfortune and the three worlds of the Trimurti would pay the price in the advancing epochs. She refused to fade into oblivion.

2.

The Sage's Wife

Devaloka. Jyestha wiped the sweat that beaded her brow. The sun in Devaloka was temperate, yet her breath was shallow by the effort of lugging the water pot. Jyestha staggered, balancing it on one hip, stepping carefully on the polished rock. The rope around her midsection was tightly wound so that the pot would not collapse. She was late, yet again. The Sarasvati River ran tamely near the hermitages of the rishis. The highest of mothers, worthy of reverence, the Devi's bounty ensured a rich and fulfilling harvest. Her waters were potent with spiritual energy. Every sage required it for his morning duties, namely in the fire rituals to the Devas and for the abhisheka of the Shiva Linga.

Jyestha only paused a moment to murmur a hurried prayer to the morning sun, Suryadev had already yellowed. The rishis at the hermitage had a strict schedule, they arose before dawn to offering prayers to the red sun. As the rocks thinned out and Jyestha measured her clumsy stride so as to not drop the pot, she heard the sound of laughter.

A woman? Surely all the sages' wives are busy in their morning chores. There is so much to do, sweep the yard, bathe the cows, prepare the oblations for the sacred fire...

"You surely jest, my lord." The woman's laughter was akin to a young girl.

Confused, Jyestha scanned the riverbank. She could not see anyone. A moment later there was a break in surface of the river's currents. Jyestha's eyes were arrested by the sight of the lovely young apasara. The heavenly nymphs. These entertainers of Indra's court were adept dancers and masters of seduction. They certainly had well-endowed forms and could even charm the heart of the most hardened rishis. Dussaha had told her to be wary of them. Yet, Jyestha stood transfixed, as though under a spell.

The apasara's wet raven locks offset her golden skin. Her eyes were the color of the deepest waters. She was lovely in every shape and form. A second head bobbed beside the female. A gandharva? Jyestha could instantly tell due to his handsome stalwart features. Seeing gandharvas and apasaras was not far-fetched, the nearby woodlands and snowcapped peaks that bordered the perimeter of the Sarasvati River were full of divine beings. These heavenly musicians and dancers resided in Devaloka. Jyestha stared openly as the pair frolicked in the water.

How easy their life is. They don't have to wake before sunrise to fetch water.

Jyestha startled at the realisation. Oh. She had to hurry. It was nearly noon by the time she reached the hermitage. Dussaha's face contorted into a permanent scowl, but her husband never scolded her for her tardiness.

"You're back." He said curtly as Jyestha busied herself in her morning duties. Their cottage was a secluded one, not too near the habitations of the other rishis. Perhaps this was due to respect for the privacy of the newly-weds. Jyestha knew it was due to fear. She braided her hair into her usual bun, tightened the coarse, homespun *uttariya* and lit the *Grihapatya* fire. The first fire to light after the *Ahvaniya*, the sacred fire of the Devas which burned endlessly in a fire pit located in the north-eastern corner of their courtyard.

Sacred fires were passed down after marriage, where the kindling wood from the family fire was used to light the new one. Dussaha silently took a firebrand from the Grihapatya fire, and used it to light the ancestral fire, in the southern corner of the yard. Replenishing and keeping the tradition of lighting the three fires was mandatory for the householder sages.

Jyestha blew into the flames with a hollowed pipe until the flames roared and then fetched the rice that she was to cook for the oblation. The water tanks were filled. Jyestha was relieved that Dussaha had no cows that she would be forced to tend to, having her hands smeared by cow dung and bathing the cattle was hardly a task that she welcomed. She had already swept the courtyard and inlaid it with auspicious *kumkum* designs. As the rice and milk was set to boil to prepare *payasa*, Dussaha made an observation.

"You took longer than usual." His tone was calm, but the question underneath was direct. Jyestha paused. Dussaha's dark eyes bore into her soul, reading its secrets. Jyestha frowned.

"I ran into an apasara and gandharva sporting at the riverbank. I scolded them and sent them away. They should not linger near our hermitages." Jyestha's half-truth did not register in Dussaha's expression. His face remained stoic as he offered rice grains in prayer to the sacred fire. Jyestha cooked outside, since she couldn't stand the smoke that stung her eyes in the cramped cottage. The other thing she could not stand were the fumes of the cow dung cakes offered in the sacred fire.

Jyestha stirred the rice and milk mixture, letting it simmer. She ducked into the cottage to fetch the jaggery from the stores. The first few days Jyestha had held her nose under her veil as she chanted mantras with Dussaha. When her husband found out he seemed displeased by her reaction. However, he said nothing. After it, Dussaha would tend to the fire ritual alone. The thatched cottage was two roomed. The antechamber served as a storeroom and the main chamber was where the couple slept. The scent of sandalwood and fresh jasmine lingered in the cottage. Jyestha returned to the simmering porridge and added the jaggery, stirring it continually to avoid splitting.

"They are doing the task that is meant for them. You should not treat them harshly. In the cosmic realm, even an ant has a purpose." Jyestha pulled the red veil over her face to hide her scowl. Dussaha had the habit of becoming a preacher during every conversation. True, he'd gained knowledge due to his penance, however Jyestha could not help wonder what was the point of all this drudgery.

Her thoughts like the bent of a river flowed back to Lakshmi. As the mistress of Vaikuntha, she would not have to do menial tasks. Even the apasaras and gandharvas fared better, they lived without fetters akin to the parrots and cuckoos that sang in the woods. They knew passion, adventure and arts. An impertinent question burned at the tip of her tongue like a firebrand.

"What's our purpose then, my lord?" Jyestha could not keep the bitterness from her tone. "We have neither riches nor glory, we live an austere life to what end? My lord told me that the material life is an illusion. That was the first lesson you taught me."

During Jyestha's first night as a bride in the hermitage, everyone had welcomed her. She was decorated with flowers and scents, auspicious lamps were waved in front of her face and her footprints dipped in red *kumkum* adorned the threshold of the cottage. Jyestha had been fully prepared to refuse Dussaha. She would not yield herself to an old man. However, the bridegroom asked nothing of her, and instead bestowed upon her a maxim in his low gravelly voice.

"The life lived in this physical body is an illusion, Jyestha. The sensory pleasures and omnipotence of power experienced in this world are temporary. I do not wish to engage myself in it for this '*maya*' is a temptress. I live with my mind fixed on Mahadeva with the hope that my soul might merge into his divinity. Do not expect the impossible from me."

Internally, Jyestha was relieved. Outwardly, she displayed her spousal anger.

"Is it because I'm not comely, my lord? Like Ahalya of old?" A thorn pricked her heart. The insecurity of her appearance reared its head. Her eyebrows furrowed in indignation.

"No, it's not like that. You're aware then, how that story ended. Ahalya still awaits her salvation. I married you because—"

"Because you pitied me." An argument on her first night. Jyestha was sure that if anyone was eavesdropping, the news would spread. However, her anger was not misplaced.

"What use is a husband if he cannot do his duty to his wife? I know some scripture as well." Jyestha countered haughtily. Sure, Dussaha was an old man, but sages were known to have the power to assume any forms. Why had he married her and cursed her to live without conjugal bliss?

"I married you because I can see the beauty of your soul. You are verily like Sri." These words did not flatter Jyestha. The mention of her sister from her husband's mouth fanned her jealousy and ire. Jyestha scowled. Her expression darkened in the light of the flickering lamp. The perfume of the flowers grew cloying.

"My lord, you admit you wanted to marry my sister Lakshmi? Are you nursing the wound of not being her Lord? Is that why you married me, as a consolation?" Her words were sharp poisoned darts that made Dussaha leave the bridal room. They had slept in different rooms that night.

In the present moment, Jyestha served the hot *payasa* in almond bowls as an offering to the sacred fire. She thought about their previous interaction. Dussaha had not yet answered her query. Perhaps he was fearful that it might spiral into an argument? Could it be that her husband was afraid of her? Jyestha snickered. After prostrating and offering oblations in the fire, she moved to the Linga made of polished stone, pouring the *abhisheka* of milk and water. This was the only activity Jyestha liked.

It was as though her essence was being purified as the water cascaded on the Shiva Linga. No thought buzzed in her head then, neither was she disturbed by the ambient sounds. Her very soul withdrew itself into a single scintillating point.

May I get a better husband in my next birth.

Jyestha sharpened this plea akin to a sickle on a whetstone. A lord of the world. Dussaha might deride power and wealth as '*maya*', however they were vital for one's sustenance in the material world. Jyestha thought about her sister again. Did Lakshmi miss her? What was she doing right now? What was the view like from her crystal palace? Once the abhisheka was done, Jyestha withdrew to the burning Grihapatya to prepare lunch. She wasn't that good of a cook, but it was better than the boiled roots and fruits that had reduced Dussaha to skin and bone. Jyestha loved peppered khichdi. She liked to prepare it and eat it in great quantity with a squeeze of lime sourced from the nearby tree.

Dussaha always raised his concern on how too much excessive eating would dull her mind, but he found fault with Jyestha's sleeping habits as well. Jyestha found that after fanning Dussaha to slumber, *Nidra Devi,* the goddess of sleep neglected her. Jyestha would sneak out of the cottage and roam the hermitage, finding some semblance of peace in the quiet of the night. At times there was this strange scent, that lured her to the banks of the Sarasvati, where she tarried endlessly looking for its source.

It was not far-fetched that someone in the hermitage had snitched.

The wives of the sages often kept their distance. Through observation and inference, Jyestha deduced that Dussaha, while revered was unpopular because he'd married her. Jyestha remained excluded from their social invitations. However, there were one or two that tried to get to know her. Vrinda and Malati. The two sisters married Sage Urdhva, and it confounded Jyestha how they managed to stay united.

The time after lunch was the only moment the women could spare to commune in the lush forest, to gather firewood for the next morning's store. Jyestha threw on her veil and hurried to meet them. The foliage surrounded her on all sides, the scent of the vegetation permeated the air. The ground was cool underfoot, the creepers and vines flowered perennially.

"Jyestha, you were late again in the morning, weren't you?" Vrinda joked. Fair-faced and pretty, Vrinda talked fast as her hands expertly chopped the firewood. Jyestha hacked at the sticks almost lethargically, she let out a tired yawn. Malati resembled her sister, but she was skinnier and nimble footed. The two were *devakanya*, or daughters of devas. Malati noticed Jyestha's yawn.

"Devi, you haven't slept properly, did something happen?" Jyestha ignored the question. She liked the sisters because they could not keep their mouths shut and they liked to gossip about the on-goings in Devaloka. Jyestha also liked them because they addressed her as Devi.

"You've been roaming too much at night. Are you seeing someone else?" Jyestha's sleepy gaze shifted from one fair face to another. She rubbed an eye.

"No. Who else would I see, besides my lord husband?" Jyestha commented.

"The gandharvas and yakshas in these woods are seducers of women. Our lord husband has cautioned us well." Vrinda murmured. Jyestha rubbed her temple.

"Perhaps your husband should be more wary of the apasaras."

Vrinda and Malati laughed at Jyestha's pointed remark. Jyestha began hacking at the wood again. The sickle made swift work of the small branches. Malati paused as she sheaved the cut-up sticks.

"Have you heard? Asura Rahu is dead. Lord Vishnu beheaded him for trying to drink the amrita. The Asura King Virochana must be very displeased. Rahu was one of his finest generals. Virochana has had a long-standing grudge against Lord Indra."

Jyestha was suddenly alert. Malati's tiny nose ring glittered in the dappled sunlight.

"Tell me everything." Jyestha mopped her brow and sank down onto the grass with her back against the trunk. Lord Vishnu beheaded Rahu? Which meant Virochana would not spare Lord Vishnu either if he decided to fight back. Jyestha's lips uplifted into a crooked smile. That meant Lakshmi would be uneasy. In that crystal palace surrounded by the ocean of milk, her sister's mind might be wracked with tension. Jyestha stared at her upturned palms. Suddenly, the calluses that had hardened on them did not appear painful.

"Why would the Lord risk Virochana's ire? Virochana is the son of his devotee Prahlada." Jyestha pointed out. Did her brother-in-law bank on Prahlada's affection? To neutralize a powerful enemy like Rahu meant inviting a war. Her mind was racing. Was there a way to manipulate this situation?

"Lord Vishnu is infallible. Indra depends on him. Virochana can do nothing, while he has a great army, Guru Shukracharya's *mritasanjivani* will not revive the Asuras due to the curse given by the Guru himself." Vrinda speculated. The *mritasanjivani* was a magical spell that the Asuras used to revive the dead comrades that had died in various mishaps.

"Virochana might perform penance to gain new powers." Malati murmured. In the grove the three women absorbed the information in silence. "Who cares? The Deva and Asura lokas are always shifting in the balance of power. As long as Lakshmi remains by her Lord's side, the Devas will never lose. We have nothing to worry."

Jyestha remained silent. If Virochana declared war, Devaloka would collapse. The sages and their wives would be harassed by the Asuras. And after something like that, no one would want those women back. The devakanya's were right to worry. Mildly disturbed by the news, Jyestha and her companions finished their duties in silence and wended their way home before dusk. The bells tied on the necks of cattle resounded in the forests as the shepherds led the animals back to their sheds. There was a subdued air about the hermitages today, even the evening prayers whose loud chanting echoed from the banks of the Sarasvati were hushed. The women moved erratically, finishing their evening duties of offering oblation to Surya.

The inside of Jyestha and Dussaha's cottage smelt stale. Jyestha did her bit to spruce up and enliven the interior with fresh jasmine before she lit the fire to prepare dinner. Boiled roots and watered down payasa was not enough to satisfy Jyestha's hunger. It did not help that worry stoked the fire in her belly, nor did it help that their stores were meagre. When Dussaha returned from the riverbank, his expression was a stony as ever. Jyestha adjusted her veil to take a look. The wrinkled lines on Dussaha's forehead did not encourage her. Dussaha combed his fingers through his beard as he was wont to do when he was distressed.

There was a slosh of water as he washed his hands and face with the water, he carried in his waterpot. Silence reigned. The earth sent out a faint scent of petrichor as it was misted, the wood in the mud kiln crackled and split. Jyestha stirred the milk porridge and turned over the roots. The sky often remained clear in Devaloka. The luminaries shone with a divine light. Jyestha shivered, cleared her throat and began rather timidly, "Did you hear the news, my lord? Asura Rahu is dead." Dussaha grunted. As dinner was served, he took his seat on the wooden pedestal and ate while Jyestha watched. Her stomach was rumbling. She resisted the pang.

"I heard. Sage Urdhva informed everyone. Lord Vishnu beheaded Rahu for drinking the amrita meant for the Devas. The Asuras attempted to steal the amrita from Dhanvantari. Lord Vishnu realised this could exacerbate the problems of the Devas. He adopted the form of Mohini, a beauteous lady and tricked the Asuras into parting with the *amrita.* Rahu doubted Mohini's intentions and assumed the form of a Deva, receiving his share. After Rahu fell beheaded by the divine Sudarshana chakra, he didn't die. He had already drunk the *amrita*, however Lord Vishnu cursed him to become a planet. Soon after that, the fighting broke out between the Devas and Asuras. However, for now, the Asuras have been defeated."

Jyestha absorbed the news in utter silence. The Devas and the Asuras were always at war for the post of Indra, the king of the gods. The seat of the Indra was coveted by the Asura kings, due to their enmity towards their cousins the Devas, due to the feud between Diti and Aditi. Each wanted to be the mother of powerful sons. Jyestha kept her thoughts to herself. She could foresee that Asura Virochana would be looking for an opportunity to strike back. A blow like this, being deceived by the Devas and having his general snatched by Lord Vishnu would mean Virochana would act soon. Jyestha surmised it would be wise to leave Devaloka in case of a war. In the skirmish between the Devas and Asuras, Jyestha did not want to become a casualty.

"How did the lord adopt the form of a beauteous lady?" That was the question that piqued her curiosity. Dussaha coughed. Jyestha bore his penetrating gaze again, hurriedly averting her eyes. Perhaps her husband had guessed her thoughts?

"Do not be too curious about the powers of the Devas. It's not something that one should employ to deceive others." Jyestha nearly scowled. She sensed the impending lecture. "Then you agree that the Devas use deceit to stay in power? Why would you waste your life in penance in their worship?" Somehow Jyestha's talks often turned incendiary. Dussaha glared as though she had poisoned the payasa.

"You talk like one influenced by Carvaka. To even listen to you is a folly." Dussaha rose from his half-finished meal with a flourish. This was the rare moment where she'd seen him lose his temper. Jyestha opened her mouth to argue but her rumbling stomach diverted her attention. She huffed, finally! Jyestha ate the remains of the payasa from the pot, but it did nothing to satisfy her hunger. Once she was finished with the chores, she went to the sleeping room. Dussaha was fast asleep by then. Jyestha lay down on her side on the mat of woven kusha grass and thought about how Lord Vishnu could adopt a charming form. What did her sister Lakshmi think about it?

The power of the Devas... well, aren't I a Devi? Can I too change my appearance as per my will? No...no, my lord will expire of a shock if he sees a beautiful lady sharing his bed. At his age it's not wise to play such a prank...

Jyestha tossed and turned, staring at the ceiling of the thatched roof. Various thoughts swirled within her mind. In the eventuality of a war, what was the best course of action? Could Virochana ever amass powers to rival Lord Vishnu? Jyestha wondered if there was a way. If she were to adopt a beautiful form and trick Virochana into being her lord...perhaps she could influence him. The Asuras were weak for beautiful women. They kidnapped many such beauties from the gardens of Indra's palace and once a woman was kidnapped, no one wanted her back. Jyestha detested this treatment of women, however she could see how it could be used in ones favour.

Well, no Asura is going to kidnap me from this unbearable sage. I better stop thinking uselessly. Virochana was afraid of me when I emerged.

Yet when sleep didn't claim her and she remained awake, Jyestha rose from her bed. She left the hermitage to go to the banks of the Sarasvati. In the darkness, the waters appeared forbidding. Jyestha gathered some of the water in the small water pot, the spare kamandalu that Dussaha used. Sages used the waters to curse or to bless others, Jyestha figured that the powers were in the water of the Sarasvati. If the Devi blessed her, she could do this. The self-awareness of her own power that lay dormant had only knocked when Dussaha had told her about Mohini.

Jyestha concentrated on her appearance in the still water of the kamandalu. She hated her prominent nose. She hated the harshness of her voice. She thought about a picture of beauty, the apasara that swam in the river. Of her raven locks, of her sea blue eyes, the soft skin that appeared like milk and her voluptuous form.

A moment of intense concentration later, Jyestha sprinkled the water on herself. Her fingers shook, more due to the anticipation than the frigidity of the water. She didn't want to open her eyes. She felt like herself, nothing felt out of place. A few moments later Jyestha's eyes opened, and she stared at her face in the still water of the kamandalu. Sea blue eyes and raven locks. An aquiline nose. Her milky skin shimmered in the light of the waning crescent and when Jyestha laughed, her voice had changed. It rang out sweetly, holding a note of melody. It was a laugh of triumph.

It rang out over the banks into the night sky and perhaps, even her sister Lakshmi might hear it ring in her palace halls. Jyestha laughed until the magic wore off and her original features returned. She would practice from now on. Dussaha did not need to know.

3.

The Ashvatta Tree

"They are asking us to leave."

Jyestha paused in the middle of sweeping. Her back was bent, she panted a little as she swept the courtyard of their cottage. Lately, she forced herself to wake early and perform her duties on time, because she practiced her shape-shifting magic in the afternoon. Vrinda and Malati were spellbound. They were her real teachers who taught her the specifics of control. The devakanya's were indispensable to Jyestha's improvement where she could sustain her illusion for longer periods of time. The women were well versed in Natya Shastra, the art of dramatics, ensuring Jyestha learned how to act the part than merely imitate it.

When the words registered in Jyestha's head, the broom slipped from her hands clattering on the neatly swept courtyard. Jyestha straightened her back, her eyes flitted to Dussaha who fiddled restlessly with his sacred thread. The wrinkles on his forehead were prominent and he combed his fingers through his beard. Jyestha watched, a trickle of sweat slunk down her jaw. She dabbed at her perspiration.

"What do you mean, my lord?" Jyestha whispered.

"The sages in the hermitage have asked us to leave." The terseness in her husband's tone made Jyestha flinch. She drew the veil upward, watching open mouthed as he put out the sacred fire. “Leave? Why, all of a sudden?” For a moment a a cold sliver of guilt bubbled within her heart. It was because of her, wasn’t it? Did the sages discover that Jyestha was using her magic? Did Vrinda and Malati...no. For some reason she wanted to trust in her sakhi’s. They would never speak for the fear of being implicated.

Jyestha, Vrinda and Malati did not merely help Jyestha practice her magic, Jyestha also roamed the woods around the Sarasvati, fooling the gandharva’s and the yakshas. The three women had the tendency to make fools of the divine beings, secure in the knowledge that they were protected due to their husbands being sages. None of the yaksha’s or gandharvas would dare to insult them, for a sage’s curse could trap them in misfortune. The victims would humbly beg for forgiveness and leave.

“They say you are the Devi of misfortune and discord. The other women are influenced by you. They’re neglecting their duties because I have been lenient to you for so long.” Dussaha was never the one to mince his words. The truth he spoke was sharp as the needles of kusha grass. “Do women not have minds of their own? If they have been neglecting their duties, it’s because of their own will.” Jyestha didn’t bother to point out that the sages often obsessed over the ‘purity’ of their wives’ conduct. The rigorous schedules were just a means to keep the women busy, allowing them no freedom. Vrinda and Malati were exceptions because Sage Urdhva often travelled away from Devaloka and there was no one around to dictate their activity. Jyestha often wished the other women would associate with her, yet they kept to their business-like cows to their sheds and calves.

“I am not leaving. Not unless, the sages come here and explain why they are ousting us as if we are diseased.” Jyestha planted her feet in the courtyard of the cottage. Dussaha glared at her as though she were a petulant child. “I am prepared to debate with them over this obtuse logic that women are corrupted due to my presence, I—"

"What did you do?" The question stung harder than any slap. Dussaha's voice was never raised, however his tone was accusatory. The dark eyes smouldered akin to hot coals. Jyestha took a step back, her face shadowed with guilt.

What did you do? I...

"My lord! You think..."

I cannot defend myself. How much does he know about what Vrinda, Malati and I have been doing? Should I lie? Does he suspect me?

"It does not matter. We are leaving this instant. A wife follows her husband's dharma without question. I shall not stay in Devaloka when the sages have questioned my honour as a rishi." The firmness in her husband's tone made Jyestha seethe with anger. Anger at her husband, at the sages, at the women...at Lakshmi. Somehow, her first thought would be directed to her sister. Why had she insisted on Jyestha's marriage and left her with no choice? Her anger bubbled like poison within her gut.

"Pack your things." By the time Jyestha realised that Dussaha was not going to change his decision, her husband had already gathered his possessions. She stared, with tears stinging her eyes at the mud kiln, whose fire had been doused. The courtyard that she had swept and maintained, the three fires extinguished. Her *kumkum* footprints which had been fresh months ago were now faded. How long had it been?

Jyestha took her time for granted. How many months had passed? She stared at the calluses on her palms. What was the point of this? Jyestha had been dreaming about influencing Virochana. She realised now how foolish her dream had been. As the sage's wife...as a personification of misfortune, fate only bestowed hardship in her lot. The dice had been cast the moment Lakshmi and her were born from that churning. Jyestha would live in her shadow, while her sister shone like the sun.

I thought I would hate this place. But I grew to like it. I had friends.

Silently, Jyestha packed her necessities. The dharma of a wife was to never question her husband's injunctions. Her fate was tied with Dussaha whether she liked it or not, it became so when Vasuki married her off.

May you perform your duty with your lord husband.

Anasuya and Arundhati followed their husbands, wherever they went. They bore every hardship and that became their pathway to glory. Yet, Jyestha had the premonition that Dussaha would never match Vasistha or Atri. He lacked the drive to achieve the post of a Brahmarishi, he was merely an ascetic. Without another word, Jyestha bundled the *stridhan*, her ornaments and her clothes.

She cushioned the ornaments in the red silk veil that she had donned on her wedding day, concealing them under her rough-spun clothing. She drew the water from the tanks that she'd striven to fill everyday in her kamandalu before performing a last *abhisheka* on the stone Shivlinga in the northern corner of the courtyard.

I do not know where I am going. Please bestow us your protection.

The noon day sun bore down on them as they walked out of the hermitage. Jyestha glanced back a couple times, wondering if she could spot Vrinda or Malati. No one accosted them as they walked. The tilled lanes and the backyard farms that bordered the hermitages were silent. The group of sages that had ousted them, paid no mind as though Dussaha and Jyestha were passing cattle. Women and children peeped from within their thatched huts. Jyestha knew she had never been welcomed in the hermitage but she remembered how they had treated her as a new bride. She struggled not to bare them any ill-will, however an imprecation arose within her mind.

I hope Virochana conquers Devaloka and he doesn't spare any of you. You don't deserve any happiness while I wallow in misery. None of you are true rishis. This is the second time I am being insulted. I was banished from Vaikuntha, from the splendour that should have been mine and now even Devaloka has abandoned me.

Jyestha did not cry. Her coppery eyes blazed instead as she followed Dussaha, the bundle tucked under her armpit and the kamandalu dangling in her other hand. Some drops of water spilled onto the boundary of the hermitage. As they turned towards the banks of the Sarasvati, Jyestha came across a broken mud pot lying on the shingle. The sight of it made Dussaha frown darkly. A bad omen? Jyestha ignored it. Omens were neither good nor bad, it is the value that the mind attached to them that became its signification.

"Where are we going, my lord?" Jyestha asked as they walk. The heat was stifling, and Jyestha perspired under the veil. She could only glimpse Dussaha's feet, clad with wooden clogs and the end of his yellowed *angavastra*. He answered after a moment, in his deep gravelly tone.

"Mrityuloka."

Jyestha's heart sunk. *Mrityuloka*? The realm where humans resided. While the Devas and other divine beings lived in Devaloka and the Asuras ruled Patalaloka, *Mrityuloka* was governed by Mrityu, the god of death. A mortal realm where Devas and Asuras roamed in disguise concealing themselves from humans. The race of Manu and Shatarupa populated *Mrityuloka* with their ephemeral lifespans. This realm did not have the resplendence of Devaloka nor was it shrouded in secrecy as Patalaloka. Humans lived and died there, struggled and returned. It was no place for a Devi like Jyestha, although Dussaha might find the company of sages.

"Where will we live? I won't stay in a hermitage. I have had enough of sages." Jyestha uttered firmly. The glare under her veil would sear Dussaha if he dared to look. Dussaha didn't answer. The journey to Mrityuloka was not punctuated by any stops. Her body, although divine was not used walking through the forests and on rough unpaved paths. The lanes around the hermitages were tilled and soft, even the grass in the forests that bordered the lands of the Sarasvati were gentle. The divine river tamed any fierceness in nature and Jyestha began to realise this was the tranquility they would be leaving behind. For a moment she wished to argue with Dussaha or to quietly return. The rigorousness of their journey seemed like a punishment, was Dussaha punishing her? Despite being a rishi, was there some underlying viciousness that he enjoying inflicting on her?

The more Jyestha followed him, the more she distrusted her husband's intentions. At one juncture, Jyestha's steps faltered, and she stumbled. They had covered a great distance. The kamandalu slipped from her fingers and clattered, spilling its contents on the path. Jyestha fanned herself with her veil, panting and exhausted. Her throat was parched, she felt dizzy. It was late afternoon, she was hungry and her feet ached.

"What is it now?" Dussaha grumbled.

"I'm tired, my lord..." Jyestha whispered. Dussaha muttered something under his breath and let her rest for a while in the shade of a banyan. Jyestha looked at her feet. The clogs she wore were not very durable. Her soles sported blisters and thorns. Jyestha remained silent as she tended to the cuts. Dussaha sat away from her, his expression blank, staring into the distance. The lines on his weathered face stood out even more. It was frigid under the shade of the great banyan, the birds were silent, but the squirrels chirruped. Jyestha startled as a squirrel leaped across the roots, landing near her.

"I don't have anything to feed you. But you can have some water if you wish. It's quite hot, isn't it?" Jyestha spoke to the squirrel, cupping some water in her palm and offering it to the animal. The squirrel drank it greedily. Jyestha broke into a smile. Animals did not care whether she was a Devi of misfortune or not. They didn't care about her appearance either, or whether she was born from poison. They spoke the language of compassion, that the sages often spoke about. *Karuna*. Yet...

Jyestha's eyes strayed to Dussaha, who sat stoic and unmoving resembling an unforgiving mountain. She was sure no compassion dwelt in his heart. He did not bother to tell her what act of hers had transgressed the rules of the hermitage. Jyestha surmised that someone took notice of the pranks she had played on the Gandharvas or Yakshas.

"My lord..."

"What is it?" Dussaha snapped. He had not beheld her face since they had left the hermitage, as though her image was an eyesore.

I'm hungry. But it is not the right time to say that.

"Where shall we stay when we reach Mrityuloka?" This was Jyestha's main concern. From what Vrinda and Malati had told her, the life of a sage in Mrityuloka was ever perilous. While the Sarasvati remained a fixture in Devaloka, she was capricious and wilful in Mrityuloka. The Devi abhorred the touch of humans and would withhold her bounty.

Sages wandered from one location to another living the life of a nomad, at the mercy of her water source. While Devaloka's forests had no predators, *Mrityuloka* was infested with dangers of wildlife in its dense jungles and worse still, bandits. The temperatures there were unreliable, and the seasons passed quickly. A year in *Mrityuloka* was equivalent to a day in Devaloka.

Dussaha's abrupt decision to leave did not befit a wise sage. Jyestha, though not comely was still a young woman. Her limbs still held their youth and her gait though fidgety was charming. She would not age much due to her lifespan as a Devi, but her lord husband of advanced years might not fare well in Mrityuloka.

To live in an unknown loka without the guarantee of an asylum, it makes me uneasy.

"I spoke to Rishi Markandeya. He informed me about the location of his old hermitage in the mountains of Himavat by the banks of the Pushpabhadra where we can stay, at least until I discover a suitable accommodation for you." Dussaha spoke calmly. His words effaced some of the worry within her heart. Jyestha stared at the shade of the banyan, cool and comforting. The chariot of Surya-Deva dipped towards the west, though there was still enough light, and it was still high in the sky. Dussaha dusted his yellowed *angavastra*, grunting as he stood.

"Come. We must get there before dark. We cannot light the three fires post sunset."

Jyestha dusted her garments as well and followed, replacing the veil. When had her lord husband met Markandeya, the highly esteemed rishi? Jyestha could not recall Dussaha ever speaking about it. Sages and Devas could travel from one Loka to another, however it depleted their spiritual powers. When Jyestha's feet touched the crumbly dry soil of *Mrityuloka*, a frigid wind cut through the rugged peaks of Himavat. The last rays of the setting sun rendered them gold and pink. She tarried a little at the summit feeling a heaviness in her physical body. The energy of *Mrityuloka* was dense and heavy, a heady mix of vibrations that concealed a certain sorrow. She watched the sunset, offering a water oblation by a small brook as Dussaha finished his evening prayer.

Round smooth stones littered this arid part. The sky towered on every side. Perhaps Rishi Markandeya's hermitage was nestled within these mountains. Jyestha followed Dussaha, mutely, holding her thoughts to herself. She had drawn the veil tightly around her and she kept close to her husband's undaunted strides. Dussaha walked with a purpose. As they wended their way down narrow mountain path, it grew colder. Soon the path was bordered by conifers that rose like guardians towards the starry sky. Dussaha used his *arani*, the firestick as a flaming torch. Its light played over his features and his dark eyes burned like embers.

They had walked for over an hour. The waxing crescent arose, outlining the mountains and the thick forests. Jyestha heard various unknown birds and the creak of her own footfalls made her uneasy. Anxiously, she sought out Dussaha's palm and held it. For reassurance. The old sage nearly dropped the firebrand in alarm.

"Where is Rishi Markandeya's ashram?" Jyestha whispered. Her voice was low and tense. Her husband squeezed her hand and replied taciturnly. "It is around the bend. Do not worry, Jyestha." His utterance offered her no comfort. Jyestha's eyes were wide, and they shone in the light of the firebrand. A stream, too small to be called a river flowed in a silver line as they arrived around the bend.

In the darkness a little village was illuminated by yellow lamp lights. Jyestha sighed in relief. Her stomach was rumbling. Perhaps a kind family would grant them a night's residence and then they could reach Markandeya's hermitage on the morrow. As they neared the boundary of the human settlement, Dussaha whose hand still gripped hers led her to a small space under the Asvattha tree. The heart-shaped leaves of the fig tree spun in the light wind. There was a small clay lamp near the tree which was extinguished. Dussaha lit it with his firebrand and gave her one portion of his *arani*.

"Jyestha, we cannot arrive unannounced in a human village. I shall go and enquire if there are any sages who will host us for the night. Wait here till I return. I shall look for a suitable accommodation for you." Jyestha stared at her lord husband in the flickering light of earthen lamp. Her lips trembled due to the cold. She was hungry and tired after their journey, and he was asking her to remain behind? She looked about the wilderness. Her heart pounded loudly like a drum.

"My lord...can't I come along?" She murmured.

"Look, humans can be nosy. I don't want the entire village to come enquiring about us. We are strangers here and the people of *Mrityuloka* view others with suspicion. I shall go and enquire about a good host, it's not proper to travel in the dark."

Jyestha accepted his explanation. Dussaha's face was stoic as ever and as weathered in the light of the firebrand. He ran his fingers through his beard and attempted a smile. The smile frightened Jyestha, striking like an arrow within her heart.

"My lord...!" She called out. Her heart was thudding and there were goosebumps on her skin. Dussaha glanced back.

"I'm hungry. We haven't eaten anything since we set out on our journey." Jyestha admitted. That wasn't the only thing. For some reason, she wanted to keep him talking, she needed his proximity. There was an unknown fear hammering within her gut and her mind. Jyestha could not name this fear. Should she fall at Dussaha's feet and beg him not to go alone? Vrinda and Malati, when they acted out their theatrics would often roleplay this dynamic between husband and wife. It made Jyestha laugh in the past, for its comical and absurd proportionality.

"I have some roots for the time being." Dussaha gave her the edibles from his bundle. "These should suffice till I return. Do not worry." Jyestha clutched the bundle, unable to retort or respond. The speech goddess seemed to have fled her burning tongue. Had it been any other day, Jyestha would have argued. She would have thrown a tantrum until Dussaha yielded to her demand.

"You will come back?" Jyestha asked aloud to her husband's retreating form. An owl hooted from somewhere in forest. Jyestha shivered, her ire was directed at the bird. Stupid bird. The owl was Lakshmi's steed, usually it portended good fortune. However, Jyestha immensely disliked its hooting. It sounded eerie in the night. In Devaloka when she roamed the banks of the Sarasvati, Jyestha hurried home whenever she heard the hooting. She thought of her sister Lakshmi, albeit bitterly.

She reigns as the queen of Vaikuntha while her elder sister descends from Devaloka to Mrityuloka. I hope she finds no peace and that Virochana takes Vaikuntha away from them. The Devas deserve every misfortune heaped upon them since they rejected me. I shall make them regret it.

Jyestha's virulent mind churned all sorts of possible scenarios for the downfall of the Devas and the Asuras. While she was far out of reach of Vaikuntha, something told her that she would return to that Loka, someday. The place of one's birth was one's true mother and while Jyestha was separated from it due to her emergence from poison, the truth would never change. Vasuki was her father, but the Kshirsagara was her mother. That ocean of milk could never remain tranquil when the fates between the two sisters was so divisive. Poison or nectar, a mother's bosom was all accepting and wept equally for their daughter's fate.

As Jyestha pulled the thin veil about her and huddled under the whispering hollow of the Asvattha tree, the leaves spun. The flame of the clay lamp guttered but it did not die out. That flame kept her hope burning much like Dussaha's firebrand. Jyestha ducked once or twice to see if she might hear his approaching footsteps, however it was silent. She fidgeted restlessly, rocking against the cramped space, startling at the slightest sound. Her stomach rumbled even more. She ate the nasty-tasting roots and drank what remained in her kamandalu.

"What's taking him so long?"

Jyestha yawned. She smelt the delicious scent of khichadi, with peppercorns and a squeeze of lime. Far off she heard Vrinda and Malati's laughter as they beckoned her. The gurgle of the Sarasvati echoed in her ears, and she smelt the scent of the three fires stoked by cowdung. The scent of the evergreen woodlands and the teasing timbres of Yaksha's and Gandharvas were heard. To top it off, there was that strange fragrance. Jyestha's nose quivered. It beckoned her to follow. Jyestha heard the splash of water about her soles and awoke with a start.

The morning fog stole over her barely concealed form. Jyestha exhaled. Her body was cold. The little lamp had gone out, having eaten up its share of oil. Jyestha used the fallen leaves of the Asvattha as fuel and lit a small fire with her arani. She warmed her hands and looked about. Where was her husband? Her eyes darted and she tried to calm her useless anxiety.

I will return. He promised me. Wait, did he?

Jyestha sat there until the morning sun pierced the thick veil of fog. There was not a soul around her. The inhabitants of the village were still asleep. Jyestha's eyes glistened with stunned tears. Her throat was choked she could not cry out.

My lord has deserted me.

4.

Mrityuloka's Trials

The life an abandoned woman is worse than that of a stray dog.

That formed the basis of Jyestha's profound realisation in the days that followed. To have a lord and yet face the sting of rejection was equal to death. The dab of *sindura* in the parting of her hair, the sacred vow of the *Prajapatya vivah* was void. Jyestha refused to believe as she lingered under the Asvattha tree that Dussaha would never return. That the trip to *Mrityuloka* was not because he wanted to live a better life, but because he wanted to unburden the source of his problems.

Jyestha realised the core of her own weakness. She had become too comfortable in the security of this marriage contract. Though their marriage wasn't perfect, it gave her status. Without it, Jyestha's identity was limited to the suspicious stares of the village women and men. The questions that some of the mortals asked her were downright humiliating.

Where is your lord husband? Who are you? Did you commit some sins, is that why your lord has deserted you? Did you give yourself to someone other than your lord? Are you a widow? Do you have any male relatives?

Jyestha, frightened by the constant questioning remained bereft of speech. What was she to say? When she tried to enquire about

Dussaha, none of villagers had ever heard of him. They seemed to show her some pity when they learned she had been a sage's wife, however, their *karuna* was superficial. It was limited to bringing her food and water, simply because if something happened to her the villagers did not want to accept the blame. The women discussed her appearance and the intricacies of her varna openly while Jyestha went about morning routine. Human society was divided into four varnas. The *brahmans* (priests), the *kshatriyas* (warriors), the *vaishyas* (tradesmen) and the *shudras* (servitors).

Jyestha listened to the talks of the women, who speculated that she merited respect as a *brahman's* wife. The other side argued that there was no proof of what *varna* she had been at her birth. Jyestha though prone to temperamental displays, remained mute and withdrawn. She withheld her true opinions and nursed the hurt that Dussaha had dealt her sharper than the bite of a Naga.

At times she would curl up under the Asvattha and weep ceaselessly ignoring food or drink. Her appearance grew unkempt, and she neglected her personal grooming. After a few weeks, even the village women stopped visiting and the men would cautiously avoid her path. She existed like an afterthought, while the only question that rattled within her mind was *why*?

The nights were freezing and restless. Jyestha stayed awake huddled near the fire that she made from the leaves of the Asvattha tree. The tree became a source of comfort for her. It asked her nothing and did its duty like a Brahmarishi. She had stashed her valuables in its hollow, more as an offering than anything else. The bundle held no meaning to her.

She knew that her father Vasuki, though he was the co-ruler of Patalaloka would not take her back. She intended to starve herself to death. Perhaps Mrityu the god of decay might spare her some compassion. But could a Devi's lifespan end in such a manner? Jyestha felt as though the Goddess of Fate had cursed her. She was ill-omened, inauspicious and the deity of discord. Humans feared her, Devas and Asuras rejected her. Dussaha abandoned her.

Perhaps it is time that I enact my role. If this Brahmanda is an ongoing stage-play, then it deserves a befitting villain. I will provide the chaos that the Devas require.

On a crisp new morning, as the cuckoo burst out into song, Jyestha purified herself at the little stream that her and Dussaha had glimpsed when they had descended the mountain. She spent hours in the freezing current, trying to collect her thoughts. Should she still don the *tilaka* of a married woman or should she renounce it? Should she keep the red veil or cast it off? While languishing under the Asvattha tree, Jyestha's heart had been numbed, yet her mind was sharp as a blade of kusha grass.

The *saubhagyavatis*, the married women donned the veil and the *tilaka* and always seemed to be in a state of anxiety. The *veshyas* who roamed sans the veil, heavily perfumed and bejewelled with different men were sluggish and pleasure seeking. They seemed to be an extension of the *apasaras* and served the purpose of entertaining the men in the human world. The third category of women were *tapasvinis*, donning deer bark and *rudraksha* as ornaments who performed penance in the mountains of the Himavat. They spoke little, seemed strict and tenacious only to their vows. Jyestha had been counseled by all three.

The saubhagyavatis told me that my fate was not in my hands and that I should return to my father. The veshyas opined that I should make good use of my freedom and secure another husband. The tapasvini's claimed that I should dedicate myself to a life of chastity and pursue my salvation at the feet of the divine.

Jyestha swam under the freezing current, before she came up for air.

But the only life that appeals to me is that of a rajapatni. My desire is to become a queen of a mighty kingdom and rule. If my sister

Lakshmi can rule Vaikuntha, why can I not find acceptance as a queen?

Mrityuloka was the crown jewel of rising and falling kingdoms. Empires rose and fell here as per the passage of time. Jyestha felt as though she should strive to create a castle in the sand. The first thing she created was a Shivalinga. Jyestha worshiped the Linga with great devotion after her morning ablutions, focusing on her goal.

I do not know why I was abandoned. I know that I have not done anything wrong so far. However, for the things I am about to do, I hope you, Mahadeva will understand my motives.

Jyestha changed her form as the fog dispersed, to that of the comely apasara that had become her muse. In her new disguise she attracted attention and even respect as she walked the path that led into the village. Whispers buzzed and Jyestha inwardly smirked. How easy it was to deceive humans. It was easier still to gain an entrance in human homes in this disguise. Jyestha amplified her charm with her magic and acting skills. She noticed how the women that had avoided her previously were now eager to serve her, to welcome her due to her appearance, her perceived status and her charming speech. The divide between what constituted as auspicious and inauspicious was like night and day. Jyestha, however, was like twilight and as changeable as the wind.

She narrated a sob story where it suited her interests, shedding pearly tears. Other times she spoke like a wise woman, bestowing advice and acting as a well-wisher. She could embody every character she chose, gradually poisoning the minds and hearts of the women with her manipulation. A woman was the mistress of the house, the very seat of power. Jyestha would show the three worlds, what could happen when that power was disrespected. She did not attach herself to these households, dividing the families, seducing the men. Jyestha never used her body. She used her words to sow seeds of doubt between husband and wife, parents and children, and the neighbours.

Soon, my sister might hear of my deeds, I will remind her that I am her elder.

The households she destroyed were the ones most devout, the ones who prayed endlessly to Lakshmi for prosperity and good fortune. When she heard the women weep and curse the goddess, when their faiths were shaken and uprooted like saplings, Jyestha felt an inner peace. If Lakshmi was going to rule, she would make sure that her sister did not have an iota of respite. Jyestha was often abused and kicked out after her machinations were discovered, but it did not affect her at all. What would the goddess of fortune do, when her devotees suffered in this way?

Jyestha had no remorse. She roamed about from village to village, adopting different forms in the mountains until discontent and discord overflowed from once prosperous and peaceful houses. The only places she didn't touch were the already degenerate ones, the gambling dens, the pleasure houses and the taverns. They did not need her chaos, the lives of these people were already sunk into a hotbed of *adharma*. For them Jyestha nursed a rare shred of sympathy. She could do nothing for them as a Devi, nor could she uplift them if she chose.

Jyestha thought about the feud between the Devas and Asuras in her free time. In *Mrityuloka*, it was impossible to weasel any information about what was happening in those domains. Humans remained unconcerned and unaware of the transference of divine beings in their own Loka and those beings were already afraid of her. Yet, Jyestha's intuition told her that someone would send an emissary. Or perhaps her sister herself would grace her with an audience.

Jyestha never failed to light a lamp before the Asvattha tree. The tree had been her only solace. When she sometimes sat under its shade, she felt immense peace. No matter how much chaos her actions spread like a mountain fire, the Asvattha tree was cool and inviting. She did not spend too much time under it for the doubt that someone clever would deduce her true identity. Her bundle still rested in its hollow. One evening, as Jyestha lit the little lamp with her *arani*, supplying the oil that she had borrowed from her latest victim, the wife of a wealthy tradesman, Jyestha heard a voice.

"May you always remain in prosperity." Jyestha raised her head. It was old and frail woman. She appeared destitute, wearing faded ochre robes. There were no ornaments on her person, though her hair was neatly tied in a single braid. Was this woman observing a vow? Women wore a single braid when in penance, especially if they awaited the return of their husbands. Jyestha could not discern the mark of any *tilaka* on the woman's silvery parting. No one would give her a second glance, much less approach. Humans took to those that displayed familiarity with their customs. This strange woman with heavy wrinkles on her face, leaning on a staff appeared confounding. Jyestha was unable to discern her status.

"I don't have any alms." Jyestha replied in a haughty voice. She had practiced the tone of authority that intimidated any unwanted attention. Jyestha learned quickly that a beautiful woman, especially if she appeared to be from an affluent household was often pestered for charity, sacrifice or manipulated into parting with her coffers. Jyestha had essayed the role of a beggar as well, so she merely ignored the mendicant woman. Jyestha's gold bangles jingled as she adjusted her veil over her head. She still sported the *sindura* of married woman despite Dussaha's abandonment. The light played on her beautiful features.

"Consider me your *anujaa*, my lady." Jyestha felt a prickle of irritation. Younger sister? What a pain. Jyestha's back straightened and her voice grew curt. "I do not have a younger sister. Please go away. Do not beg at the auspicious twilight hour like an '*alakshmi*.'" Jyestha's tongue held a bit of venom. That remark often had singed her deeply during her initial forages for food and shelter. Jyestha had never been welcomed at twilight in her true form in any of the mountain villages.

Jyestha rose after her brief prayer. She dusted her expensive robes, wending her way to the house of the new victim. Her gait was poised and precise and she walked with confidence. The target she had chosen resided at the foothills where the hamlets converged with towns. Jyestha showed no sense of fear as she traversed the path, guided by the light of her firebrand.

It was risky to come all the way here. If the people of the foothills suspected her identity, Jyestha could be cut off from the prosperous districts where she could swindle more families. Jyestha discovered early on that when she spread her roots of discord within people, the prosperity they earned through their nefarious means immediately transferred to her. In other words, she didn't require employment and could earn her means and operate independently as her influence grew.

Jyestha heard the tapping of the woman's stick as she was followed. A faint line of irritation creased her charming brows. Was this old woman crazy? This walk down the mountain path might kill her. Jyestha tried to ignore the woman's echoing footsteps and tried to focus on her scheme. Now how might she poison the mind of the trader's wife? She studied the workings of their household intricately.

The trader was a renowned lapidary. He and his wife were quite pious, performing many charities and sacrifices in the name of Lakshmi Devi. Jyestha's attention had been drawn to them because the trader had publicly performed a *yajna*, a fire sacrifice in the honour of the Devi, feeding many guests and giving away a wealth of cows to sages. The trader had two sons, though both were away at gurukul. In the present moment, she could only sow discord between the husband wife. Jyestha smirked.

Perhaps the truth that her husband is an exclusive client of the pleasure houses at the outskirts of the district might be the right seed. No woman would tolerate such an ignoble sin.

As Jyestha thought about how she would broach the topic to her new victim she heard the tap of the stick and the sound of someone falling. Jyestha startled by the sound whirled around. The persistent old woman, pursuing her like a wasp pursued the lotus had collapsed. Serves her right, who in their right mind would make such an arduous descent at her age?

"*Agrajaa*, can you lend me a hand?" Jyestha paused. *Agrajaa*, the one who walks before me. An epithet for an older sister, similar to her real name, Jyestha. Jyestha's heart lurched. She averted her gaze, but the old woman, having had such a fall in the middle of the wilderness appeared helpless. No traveller would stop by at this hour of the evening. Humans were a superstitious lot, believing in the wrath of *bhutas* and *pishachas*, the goblins that accompanied Mahadeva. Frightened easily by humans that strayed from the social order, not one would help this woman. Jyestha cursed outwardly.

"At this rate you will descend into Patala, old woman. Come stand. Whose ill advice do you follow, that you are eager to fall to your death." Jyestha's tongue wagged like a sword. She braced the lady against one shoulder, pulling her towards a nearby rock. Jyestha then brought the staff back and examined the old woman's injuries.

"There's not a mark on you. You are fortunate. If it wasn't for me, no one would have helped you." Jyestha presented her kamandalu of water, which always remained full. The woman slaked her thirst. Her deep-set eyes were too kind, it made Jyestha's heart sting with unexpressed guilt at her own treatment of the woman.

"You have erased any of your sins by scolding me like an elder sister. I longed to hear such words for very long." Jyestha scoffed. She felt the heat rise to her face. She wished to extricate herself from this embarrassing situation and hurry to the home of her latest victim. "Come. It's not right for two women to tarry in the wilderness. We may be mistaken for yakshini's or worse."

Jyestha lit her firebrand again. There was a faint smile on the vagrant woman's face. In the glow she appeared benevolent, a picture of grace and dignity. Jyestha felt as though she wanted to stuff herself into a small niche and disappear. She had treated this saintly woman with disrespect. Jyestha noted the silver line of sacred thread about the woman's torso. A brahman woman? How deep of a hole should she dig for herself to slither into? Jyestha's mind was wracked by fear.

If she curses me, I'm done for. I better apologize and beg for forgiveness.

Jyestha reached to touch her feet. The woman, alarmed by her action gripped Jyestha's bedecked wrists. "No, *agrajaa*. Do not accrue me any more sins. I have been a source of turmoil for you on this pathway. Your road has been harsh and thorny because of me. Can you forgive me?"

Jyestha was taken aback by the depth of emotion in her frail cracking voice. She sighed and rose. Forgive her for being an old woman who could not walk without a staff? This woman had probably lost her senses. Jyestha rubbed her temple.

"*Anujaa*, we must not linger here. Let us reach a populated district quickly. To make it easier I will carry you on my shoulders." Jyestha did not let the old woman decide. She was frail and light, not much of a burden. Jyestha was youthful and strong, the time she spent being a sage's wife meant she had built up an endurance for labour. When the two women reached the districts, Jyestha set the old woman upright.

"Go your way. I am already late." Jyestha recollected her present mission and made her way to the trader's opulent house. Night had fallen. Humans milled in the streets, going about their business. The courtyards of the houses displayed lit earthen lamps. Mothers harked the children homeward as they finished their evening prayers. Jyestha heard the tap of the staff. She glanced at the old woman, who was still dogging her steps.

"Why are you following me?" Jyestha inquired.

"I am visiting the same house as you, *Agrajaa.* Come let us go together." Jyestha clicked her tongue. Her plan would be foiled if this lady came along. However, the fear of a curse kept her from complaining out aloud. The two women arrived at the courtyard of the trader. Jyestha peeped about anxiously. She could not enter unless the host invited her into the house. The old lady tarried beside her.

"Why don't you go in? Aren't they expecting you?" Jyestha prodded.

"Like you, I am an unexpected visitor. I shall wait to be invited."

Jyestha felt a twinge of suspicion. She kept her gaze held high, her eye fixed to the painted threshold and the decorated doorway. From inside Jyestha heard the murmur of chants as the householders worshiped the goddess of fortune. The heady scent of myrrh and frankincense wafted towards Jyestha's nose.

Her praises are being sung everywhere and I have to stand here and listen to it. How demeaning!

Jyestha realised that she was making a wry face. It did not escape her companion's scrutiny. She was bestowed a gentle smile. Jyestha smiled in return as the moments passed, the air between the visitors grew uncomfortable. Jyestha fidgeted with the drape of her *uttariya*, growing restless as her patience waned. How long would she be made to wait?

"The goddess of fortune is ever restless."

Jyestha felt the goosebumps rise as she heard her companion speak again. She tried shaking off this sense of unease. Jyestha licked her lips, her kohl lined gaze darted toward the old lady. There was a detail she had missed about her mysterious companion. Jyestha wondered how she could be this unobservant. The lady wore a single garland made of pink lotus buds. Jyestha huffed.

"Oh, it is you, *kanishtha.*" Jyestha's tone was cold and sour like a bitter lemon. "How grand of you to grace *Mrityuloka* with your divine presence." Her shoulders stiffened with righteous anger. Lakshmi had misused her karuna, her sense of compassion. Jyestha had unknowingly borne her own sister to the door of her precious devotee. Her gut simmered with rage.

"*Agrajaa*, your anger towards my devotees is misplaced." Lakshmi's dulcet tone did nothing to assuage Jyestha's flaring temper. Jyestha clenched her fist until the nails bit into her palm.

"Is it? Your devotees are double-faced. Shall I recount the sins of your precious devotees? I know them all. Or shall I spare your soft heart that is only an ocean of compassion towards those that worship you but neglect the sorrow of your kith and kin?" Jyestha's face was shadowed with malevolence. Her eyes spit fire. If Jyestha had the power of a true *tapasvini* there was no doubt she would set the three worlds ablaze.

"*Agrajaa*, I only recently came to know of your fate, it pains me".

"No. You have a heart of stone. How could you possibly understand the pain of abandonment? Your lord resides as the ruler of the three worlds, and you are never separated from him even for an instant. Do not attempt to console me with your empty sympathies." Jyestha countered with a deadly calm.

"*Agrajaa*, I would take your misfortune upon my head if you allowed me. Please do not walk down this path of destruction. You shall regret it. Allow me this mercy, of seeing your good fortune." Lakshmi's palms were joined in supplication and her head was bowed.

"*My* good fortune?" Jyestha scoffed. "You forget that I am *Alakshmi*. You have immense love for your devotees, do you not?

Then why do we not let them decide? Can they differentiate between you and me? Or are they simpletons who are deluded by auspicious and inauspicious omens?" Lakshmi's head remained bowed at Jyestha's utterance. A ripple rent through the air as the two goddesses stood.

"Obeisance to the two mothers." The trader's wife arrived at the doorway, she anointed the two women with *haldi* and *kumkum* as a sign of acknowledgement. Jyestha and Lakshmi fixed their eyes onto her. Jyestha knew that her appearance befitted a *saubhagyavati*. Lakshmi on the other hand appeared confounding, with no auspicious symbolism. Jyestha addressed the trader's wife, her voice as mellifluous as a flute.

"The two of us have heard about your great deeds, gentle one. However, we are at crossroads. So do tell, who among us is superior? Who among us is more beautiful? Who among us worthy of worship?" Jyestha spoke. The trader's wife glanced from Jyestha to Lakshmi. Her face was wrought with tension. Jyestha knew she could not offend either guest. Lakshmi's face was solemn as ever, her brown eyes gleamed as she gazed at her devotee.

"Mothers, you both are quite beautiful," The trader's wife answered. She was studying them, "however, the *tapasvini* is beautiful when she steps forward, while you, *saubhagyavati* are beautiful when you step back. The *tapasvini* is superior due to her age and her power of penance but both of you are worthy of worship." The trader's wife bowed to Jyestha and Lakshmi in turn.

Inwardly Jyestha's mind reeled with the shock of the answer. Outwardly, she smiled benevolently, stepping away from the courtyard with the offering of coconut and rice grains. Lakshmi did not smile as she stepped over the threshold basking at the welcome. Jyestha's smile disappeared as she wended past the crossroad, her heart burning with envy.

...I shall, not forget this ignominy.

5.

Gandharva Vivah

"Om Namaha Shivaya."

Jyestha sat in penance. Ever since the episode with the trader's wife and meeting Lakshmi, she had situated herself in the mountain peak of Himavat, by the Shivalinga made of sand. Her bitterness culminated into a single-minded focus. She would grow her powers through penance and obtain boons to teach the Devas a lesson. Jyestha took her oath, bearing inclement weather, hunger and thirst. She meditated on Shiva. Jyestha knew that her prayers would reach the heart of the compassionate Lord. Her body grew gaunt and weary, and she nearly reduced to skin and bone. Despite the harshness of her tapas, the Lord did not grace her with his presence.

"*Narayan, Narayan,* salutation to you, Devi."

Jyestha's shoulders stiffened. She knew the speaker. The emissary of her brother-in-law, Lord Vishnu. Narada Muni stood at a respectful distance with his head bowed. Jyestha sighed. She wished to ignore him completely and resume her meditation, but it would be difficult to concentrate if he stood there and talked. All the same, a Brahmarishi could not be ignored. Jyestha gestured to the bed of kusha grass where the sage could sit.

"I suppose my brother-in-law has sent you, revered sage."

Jyestha uttered formally. Her tone was subdued. She offered him the roots she so detested and the water from her kamandalu. Jyestha watched him partake the offering and felt the absence of hunger. These days, she felt the absence of everything except the fire that blazed within her heart. The rays of the sun did not enchant her, nor did the beauty of the mountain peaks, neither the song of birds nor the scent of charming flowers. The hair piled at the top of her head was matted and rough. Her figure had shrunk to that of an aged woman. Neither the birds nor animals stirred any joy. Jyestha felt she was an observer. She barely ever thought about Dussaha.

"You are omniscient as ever, Devi. Your incessant tribulations have moved the hearts of my lord and his consort. They are deeply affected by your abandonment. My mistress can find no peace of mind unless you find felicity."

Jyestha listened in silence. The emissary paused wearied by his eloquent speech. Jyestha showed little emotion. She nodded. Her eyes were fixed on the Shivalinga that she worshiped in contemplation.

"Lord Vishnu informed me that he has found you a suitable groom. Neither a Deva or Asura, nor a sage or a human." Narada went on. "A Gandharva called Kali, one of the few that survived the melee that occurred during Asura Rahu's death, he was present during the churning of the ocean, a fine musician and one of my dearest friends. Kali possesses the same qualities as you, Devi. He is charming and well versed in the art of dramatics, the great-great grandson of Lord Brahma. I exhort you to consider this potential match."

Jyestha blinked. She felt a dull twinge of resentment. The Devas certainly did not wish her to gain any powers, for the fear that she become unmanageable. Jyestha concealed her true thoughts from the sage, although she could guess that this might be her brother-in-law's attempt to put an end to her wayward nature.

"I shall consider your suggestion, revered sage." Jyestha ducked her head in supplication as Narada took his leave. She heard the strum of the strings of his divine veena as he disappeared from the view. Jyestha sat on the rock in front of the Shiva Linga in silence. She did not move from her position for the next two days.

Why is it when I adopt the path of a tapasvini that you must dangle the blessedness of saubhagya in my way? Mahadeva, do you not pity me?

The Shiva Linga did not render any answers. Jyestha sat alone in wilderness, detaching herself from the outcome of this decision. Kali might reject her. The progeny of Lord Brahma was known for their entitlement. Jyestha knew the story of Daksha Prajapati. Narada Muni had extolled his attributes, yet Jyestha had never heard of Kali. Among the Gandharvas, Tumburu, the favorite musician of Lord Vishnu and Vishvavasu, the king of the Gandharvas who was the consort of Apasara Menaka were the prominent ones.

Gandharvas are fond of beautiful women. Kali will not take me seriously, especially if he has witnessed my emergence from the poison. Am I a laughing stock in the three worlds?

Jyestha put the matter at the back of her mind. Though, Narada's visit ended up breaking her penance. Jyestha began to roam in the mountains and valleys again, albeit this time she avoided the villages. Jyestha's mind was confounded with doubt as she considered her options in the solitude of the Himavat. She could return to her previous ways, harass humans and deceive them or she could choose this new groom, adapt to his new lifestyle and remain content with her fate.

Jyestha's lofty aspirations had dimmed, and the outlandish plans she had devised in Devaloka seemed to be the childish fancies of an immature girl. For the first time in many months, she studied the lines on her left and right palms. Her left eyelid throbbed. An auspicious sign? Jyestha had ceased believing in such omens. Or rather she had never believed in them.

She lent any weight to Lord Vishnu's selection, only because Kali was a Gandharva. Jyestha recalled the lovely apasara and the handsome gandharva she had encountered in Devaloka while performing her duties as a sage's wife. With Dussaha, she had secretly yearned for the lifestyle of the Gandharvas, but her lord husband's eccentric ways and their incompatible natures left no room for the satisfaction of the desires of a young woman. Nor could she ever give herself to Dussaha, who shunned all material pleasures. Jyestha was not young anymore. Her hardships on *Mrityuloka* had prematurely ravaged her youth.

I will not be bound to a rigorous schedule. Perhaps the marriage to a Gandharva might not be an awful decision. I can have my free will. But how do I go about this?

If Jyestha approached Kali with the deception and charm that she exuded when she essayed her role of seductress, he might run away. Kali was surely not a fool, he would see through Jyestha's disguise. The Gandharva's possessed supernatural magics such as shape-shifting and omniscience. It would be unwise to begin with deception. Jyestha felt the trepidation swirl within her gut. An unknown fear held her back.

Of course, the first thing would be to gather information about Kali. I don't know anything about him. I wish Vrinda and Malati were here. They would have the correct advice.

Jyestha felt the prickle of her first tears as she contemplated on the banks of the river Pushpabhadra. Vrinda and Malati, how were the Devakanyas? Jyestha had not thought about them and in *Mrityuloka* she did not trust a single soul. She realised how alone she was in this realm. The tranquility of the river did not mirror the turmoil within her heart. Jyestha sobbed quietly, her vision blurring as she gazed at the mountains in the distance. It was lovely. The beautiful lilies and lotuses that blossomed in the marshes where the river flowed tamely wafted a soothing fragrance. Deer roamed in the forest, the cuckoo and parrots often burst into song to welcome the spring.

When was the last time I plucked a flower? Or the last time I properly oiled my hair?

Jyestha's eyes were arrested by the lotuses in full bloom. Among the pink and red lotuses there was a lotus that shone violet blue. It stood out due to its unusual hue. Unthinkingly Jyestha waded into the current to pluck it. As her hand reached out to pluck the lotus the current shifted as if to keep it away.

"Ah!" She cursed her fatal moment of weakness. A large wave threw her off balance. Jyestha thought she had grasped the flower, but her hand grabbed only air. As she floundered, stunned by the sudden twist of the raging water, someone grabbed her from behind. Jyestha felt herself being dragged backward. Her eyes were wide with fear. The threat of the oncoming wave made her knees buckle.

"Devi, are you trying to end your life?" Jyestha found her feet planted on dry rock. She shivered. What was she doing? For the sake of a lotus, Jyestha would have been swept away by the current and drowned in its embrace. Her heart was still hammering within her chest. She felt like an absolute fool. When the panic had subsided and she was at a safe distance from the current, Jyestha turned to thank her benefactor.

"Thank you." Jyestha began bowing her head.

"No, Devi. You must not bow your head to anyone." Jyestha's eyelashes fluttered as she glimpsed the man who had saved her life. He was tall, slender and striking. His dark hair fell to his strong shoulders. His skin shimmered like silver and gold in the sunlight that stole through the trees. But what entranced her were his eyes, they were the colour of the violet-blue lotus that she had been seeking. Previously, Vrinda and Malati had spoken about Manmantha, the god of love. If anyone could resemble a god of love, it would have to be this man.

Jyestha immediately lowered her eyes and fixed them to her feet. Her face was burning in shame. She felt the flutter in her gut and was ever more conscious of her unkempt, untidy appearance. She was aware of her matted hair, the ash and dust that she had smeared on her skin to make herself appear unappealing and her shriveled gaunt body, weary due to her rigorous penance. The sunlight highlighted her every flaw.

"Why do you stand like a criminal, Devi, have I put you on a trial?" She flinched as he draped his pure white *uttariya* about her shoulders. Jyestha shivered, due to the wind, his proximity and everything else that was rushing like the Pushpabhadra in her mind. "No." Jyestha found her voice finally and followed his steps to a clearing where the sunlight was a golden patch among a meadow of wildflowers.

"Then look up at me."

"I cannot look at any man besides my husband. I thank you for saving my life, but I should not behold your face." Jyestha murmured dryly. Of course, fate would send a temptation her way in the form of this man. Jyestha frowned bitterly wondering where her wits and her wiles had vanished. She had never been mesmerized by a human man. Perhaps this man was not human? Who was he? A Deva? Or a Yaksha?

"Devi, you surely do not believe in such lies. A *tapasvini* like you, who has cast off all desires should never be afraid of looking at anyone in the face. I am sure any man that looks at you wrongly will be burnt to a cinder."

Jyestha's confusion rose. She kept her eyes to her dirty feet, with its untrimmed nails. She still felt the tightness within her throat. This mysterious man spoke like a scholar, someone well-versed in arts and sciences.

"I take your leave. Please be careful, Devi."

"Wait." Jyestha blurted. She glimpsed his receding back. There was one thing that she still required. This time Jyestha kept her head upright. Her gaze did not waver. "Can you get me that flower? The blue lotus. I wish to offer it to my lord."

"Devi, you want me to risk my life for a lotus?" He smirked. Jyestha did not return his smile. "Not any lotus, it is a special one of an unusual color. I surmise you must be a good swimmer." Jyestha persisted.

"I am, but I don't see the point of swimming in a dangerous current to pluck a lotus for a lady who will offer it to her lord husband. Isn't that an inappropriate request?" Jyestha nearly scoffed as the stranger stood his ground. She could plainly detect that he was a Gandharva. Perhaps he roamed in these woods to charm human women.

"I meant the lord I worship. Mahadeva, the great god." Jyestha uttered with pride.

"I see. What will you give me if I get it for you? I will not work for free, Devi." Jyestha nearly rolled her eyes at his defiance. So much for his charming words and his gallantry. From what Jyestha knew of Gandharva's, they would do anything for the company of women, which led them to think less and follow their passions. This Gandharva's defiance meant he would not be easy to manipulate or command.

"What do you want?" She drew the *uttariya* he had draped about her shoulders snugly and stood tall. The sunlight glimmered over the both of them.

A companion who can play dice with me. Although, I should not ask this of a *tapasvini*." The Gandharva appeared radiant in the sunlight, an avatar of Surya himself. His form was nebulous and ever changing.

"I do not know how to play dice." Jyestha declared.

"I can teach you. I will go easy on you, Devi, though I play to win."

"How many games have you won?"

"Do you want the flower or not? I can opt to leave." He shifted and the slight tug of his mouth displayed his irritation.

"Alright. I will play dice with you, go and get me the lotus. I want it for my afternoon worship." He ducked at her command. "*Tapasvini*, you order a man about like a queen. I am not sure if I admire it or not."

Jyestha paused. She watched as he fearlessly dove into the current to get her the blue lotus. Jyestha turned her eyes to the sky. Her lips parted slightly as she noted the anomaly in the sky. Narada Muni was observing their interaction, with amusement. When his eyes met Jyestha's the messenger of Lord Vishnu joined his palms in greeting and vanished skyward. Jyestha shuddered, feeling slightly unsettled. So, then this must be...

"Here." Jyestha gazed at the blue lotus that Gandharva Kali thrust into her palm. It was matched the exact color of his eyes. Jyestha returned his *uttariya* and walked forward. He fell into step behind her at an easy pace. "You are the Gandharva Kali. The great-great grandson of Lord Brahma."

"My exploits have reached your ears? Was it the esteemed sage Narada that sang my praises?" Jyestha was taken aback by the sarcasm in his tone. They walked to the place that Jyestha lived. The little stream that was the tributary of the Pushpabhadra. Jyestha sat before the Shiva Linga and offered the flower in worship. Her eyes remained closed.

Is this the man I should marry? In the short conversation I have had with him, I like him already. Though I fear he might be sent here to tempt me.

"I am not always honest, Devi, however I wish to clarify. You exploits have reached my ears far more. Jyestha the Devi of misfortune who wed the sage Dussaha. The Devi who roamed the banks of the Sarasvati, changing her form at night. The friend of the Devakanyas Vrinda and Malati. The goddess who was a terror in *Mrityuloka* when her ire was unleashed. Truth be told, you should not waste away your potential."

Jyestha opened her eyes. Kali lit the *arani* without her insistence and took his seat on the mat of *kusha* grass. Out of thin air, a dice board materialized before him, the complete set with two silver die-heads and a number of pawns. She watched with interest as he set up the game.

"If you do not calculate your evens and odds, you shall end up on the losing side of this game. You went from Vaikuntha, to Devaloka, to *Mrityuloka*. You are descending, Devi. Do you wish to end up in Patala?" Jyestha craned her neck, watching open-mouthed as he expertly assessed each roll, and the correct value made her lose her pawns. Jyestha stared at him. His calm gaze pierced her very mind, as though he could read every concealed thought.

"Will you help me ascend?" She whispered.

"I cannot promise that. However, I witnessed your insult in Vaikuntha. Your sister reigned supreme while you suffered endlessly. I can understand the depth of your pain. If you take my hand in companionship, I will teach you a game that you can always win." Kali's eyes bore into hers and Jyestha shivered against his whisper in her ear.

"Otherwise, be content in this life of a *tapasvini*. These fruits and roots, and this solitude. Endless prayers and useless tears do not make the pathway of a ruler. What I can teach you will give you everything you desire and more, should you aspire for it. Aren't you tired of this life of insult?" Kali was speaking like a scholar, a minister of a king, Jyestha was lured by the promise of his words alone. Her heart was swayed, and her mind enraptured by the vision.

"One's birth or *varna* should not constrict one's true ambition. That is what I believe. So, what if you emerged from poison? Any individual, no matter the consequence can rise to a position of power and sustain it. I have observed Devas, Asuras and human kings. I know how to sway their mind and lure them into temptation so that they make grave mistakes." Jyestha jolted at his words. She drew back to increase the distance between her and Kali. Her heart stung by the realisation that he was manipulating her emotions.

"You are a liar." She hissed.

"Yes, I am, and I proclaim it openly, but only to you, Devi. I still firmly believe that you should never bow your head. So, shall I teach you this game? Or shall I take my leave?" Jyestha turned her face away and gazed at the twilight that descended in the mountains. The Shiva Linga glistened with the offering of the blue lotus. Jyestha felt Kali's gentle touch on her shoulder.

"Teach me." Jyestha asserted.

The light of the fire played on Kali's soft features as he smiled, a sly mischievous smirk. That night he taught her the game of dice and some other things too. At the end of it all, Jyestha only had one thought in her head.

Is this what they call Gandharva Vivah?

6.

Alakshmi's Fortune

"Correct your form, *priye.*"

Jyestha clicked her tongue. Her anklets jingled on the carpet of the opulent dance hall. The *natya-griha* was roomy and opulent. The floor was inlaid with glossy tiles. Crystal chandeliers were suspended from the ceilings. There was the pleasant fragrance of burning aloe. The figure of Nataraja, the Lord of Dance and Dramatics glimmered on a pedestal in the corner. Kali sat on a cushioned platform, absently rolling his dice. The *natya-griha* of Devaloka was Kali's favorite haunts.

"You aren't even looking at me." Jyestha pointed out as she practiced.

"I'm analysing your footwork, I do not need to look at you." Her *gandharva* husband answered. Jyestha was practicing the role of a seasoned dancer. She heard the faint murmur as the dice clattered onto the board. Jyestha's guise of a comely *apasara* shimmered and shifted as she gracefully executed a dance move.

"Again." Kali's curt tone made Jyestha wince. She rolled her shoulders. Her footsteps brushed across the soft carpet keeping time with Kali's instructions. As a Gandharva, he often corrected the form and posture of the dramatists, ensured that the actors in the *abhinaya* expressed the correct emotions according to the mood of the scene and negotiated any disagreements that broke out between the artistes.

She understood quite quickly that her new husband was a hard taskmaster. He persevered for perfection. Whether it be dance or drama, shape-shifting or the intricacies of law and politics, Jyestha had to perfect it until he was satisfied. He never asked her to sing or play an instrument, this was something Kali preferred to do by himself. Jyestha had shared her vision with him, of deceiving Virochana and orchestrating the downfall of the Devas. After it, Kali began tutoring her so that she could perfect her disguises and bring her vision into reality.

"If you're going to influence Asura Virochana, you have to act well. The Asuras are distrustful and advanced practitioners of magic. Even the slightest mistake could cost us our heads. To entice him, you have to be accomplished in every aspect and he should never suspect you." Jyestha paused her footwork. She let out a sigh. The constant roll of the dice was getting on her nerves. Her anklets tinkled as she maintained the gait of an apasara.

"My lord, what ails you?" Jyestha took her seat beside him. Her bejewelled arms reached for the box of betel nuts and leaves. Kali instructed her in the etiquette of *rajapatni's* and this was a task that Jyestha loved to do. Her past with Dussaha was already dissipating like mirage. Jyestha had learned how to dress and braid her hair into various styles, bedeck herself with flowers and perfume and wear many different costumes, thanks to the other apasaras who were eager to teach her. Kali had introduced her as his new pupil and due to his connections, Jyestha was granted favour.

At times, Jyestha's jealousy flared when the other apasaras tried to become intimate with Kali. Her jealousy would amuse him, but he took his marriage with her seriously and never transgressed the bounds of decency with the other women. At this juncture of their relationship, they had learned to read each other's moods well.

"It's nothing." Jyestha offered him the betel-leaf. Kali's blue eyes glimmered with dull frustration as he evaded her question. He reset the board with a flick of his wrist beginning a complex game. Jyestha studied his movements. Kali's moodiness had taught her the virtue of patience. As Kali played against himself, Jyestha noticed the numbers on the dice.

"You need an even throw to win, my lord." She suggested.

Kali glanced at her. A subtle smirk uplifted the corner of his mouth.

"Look again, Jyestha." Jyestha craned her neck, studying the board with intensity. She reached for the dice and rolled. The throw landed on an odd aggregate. Jyestha moved her pieces. If Kali landed an even throw, he would lose his stake. Jyestha laughed. "What sorcery is this, my lord?" She murmured, bemused.

"It is not sorcery, *priye*. It is the power of numbers. I have learned from my past to not underestimate anyone. Even the weakest number can prove beneficial and sway the tide." Jyestha listened stoically. Kali's expression was distant. Jyestha knew that once Kali sunk into the mistakes of his past, he would begin to drink. She quickly removed the decanter of Soma, the drink that the Devas and Gandharvas were fond of drinking. Her husband noticed this and grumbled.

"Do you not trust me with your worries? If you are not going to share your deepest thoughts with me, what is the use of my companionship? Didn't you say, the wife is a friend in the home?" Jyestha's words were sweet and tactful imbued with the art of persuasion. She was essaying the role of a perfect wife, sweet in speech and concerned for her lord's troubles. Kali stirred. He ended the game of dice and rested his head against her lap. Jyestha felt a twinge of pride.

"I wish I was employed in a higher station, Jyestha." Kali murmured. Jyestha ran her fingers over his dark curls. Kali's face was pale and creased with worry. As her fingers soothed his tensions, Kali began to speak. She listened to his voice with impartiality as it resounded in the opulence of the dance hall.

"I may be the descendant of Lord Brahma, but I am not respected. I have the education and the talent to aim higher, however I am taken for an entertainer. I am supposed to hover and know-tow to the likes of Indra and Virochana, dance to their rhythm like a puppet. If I was born as a Deva or an Asura, the Trimurti would hand me a dominion on a platter. Does it not frustrate you? To be the companion of a Gandharva who has no fixed station? Vishvavasu is the King of Gandharvas, Tumburu is an esteemed musician, while my close friend Dvapara is the Yuga Purusha, the lord of an epoch in *Mrityuloka*. And I? I am nothing."

Jyestha's heart lurched. Kali's voice was laden with a deep-seated resentment against his helplessness. Jyestha wondered if she should offer him a platitude. However, Kali had not married her because she could speak sweetly to him. He prized her true opinion and took it to heart.

"It does...frustrate me. Not the fact that you are a Gandharva, or the fact that I married you. It frustrates me that you and I are chasing the chariot of the sun while being blinded by its rays. It frustrates me that I am a Devi of misfortune and that I cannot add to your fortune, my lord. The wealth you earn through deception is what I can grant, yet I cannot uplift you. Perhaps this is our greatest weakness."

Kali listened to her words in absolute silence. His gentle breath fanned her lap. Then he opened his eyes, blue and despairing and let out a quiet laugh. Jyestha stared at his upturned face and smiled, her disguise faded, and her coppery eyes gleamed with contrition. Her husband ran a finger along her long nose and murmured, "We are a pair of losers, *priye*. A perfect match." Their hearty laughter rang in the dance hall.

This interaction lingered in Jyestha's mind. She thought of her sister Lakshmi after many ages. The time she had spent with Kali had been so enthralling that she had forgotten her sister. She had forgotten *Mrityuloka* and had been eager to follow along his schemes. Virochana was performing an expiation after the death of Rahu. Devaloka's tranquility remained unbroken as long as the Asura remained absorbed in his penance. Jyestha and Kali both surmised that Virochana would mobilize his forces after he gained a boon, and that the expiation was only a ruse.

In his present status, Kali would never be able to use his machinations against the higher powers. The Trimurti would not allow a mere Gandharva to meddle in the matters of the Devas and Asuras. To form powerful connections, he needed a title. A title, Jyestha could not bestow on him. Kali wanted to fulfil her dream of being a *rajapatni*, the wife of a king. However, to grant him kingship, one required Lakshmi's blessing.

Indra ruled due to '*Raja-shri*', the throne that granted him the right of authority. Lord Vishnu ruled due to '*Shri*' being his eternal consort. When Rishi Durvasa had cursed the three worlds to lose '*Shri*', Lakshmi had vanished and the social order had descended into chaos. The churning had brought her back and along with Lakshmi came the *amrita*, coveted by the Asuras who were not immortal.

Why was I born then? My existence is a curse to the people I love.

Jyestha's footsteps had taken her to *Mrityuloka*. It had been nearly seven Deva years since the churning of the ocean. In *Mrityuloka*, time passed differently. The people Jyestha had encountered during her tribulations had passed away many lifetimes ago. The passage of the Yugas meant *Mrityuloka's* laws and perceptions changed. The hearts and the minds of people also progressed from nobility to deception.

It was Deepavali. Jyestha moved about in disguise. She was not out trouble humans this time. She was observing the festivities, and the way humans decorated their homes and lighted earthen lamps to welcome Lakshmi. The familiar scent of frankincense wafted past her nose. Jyestha smiled, her heart moved by nostalgia. The essence of her bittersweet memories lingered in this Loka. Her leisurely pace took her down the mountains of the Himavat. Jyestha was curious whether she could find the Asvattha tree again. The outskirts of a familiar village approached. Glimpsing the tree, Jyestha's heart leapt. It had survived the passage of time.

If I had never come to Mrityuloka, I would not have been able to meet my lord. I faced many hurdles in this place but the bank of the river Pushpabhadra was fortunate to me. Mahadeva blessed me with saubhagya.

It was also the anniversary of her emergence. Jyestha lit a lamp under the Asvattha tree, paying her respect to whichever spirit resided there. The tree had been her friend. As Jyestha prayed, she heard a familiar voice.

"*Agrajaa.* How fortunate I am to see you. I am delighted to hear of your good fortune. Gandharva Kali turned to be a good match for you."

Lakshmi. Her twin sister was moving about *Mrityuloka* to bless her devotees. She stood smilingly before Jyestha, welcoming her openly. Jyestha returned her smile rising from her crouched posture. Lakshmi's face shone. She exuded this aura of contentment. The fabric of the pink brocade Lakshmi wore was the colour of the pink lotus. Jyestha's was a violet blue. Jyestha invited Lakshmi to take a seat.

"*Anujaa.* I hope everything is well with you." Jyestha sat on the stone platform constructed around the Asvattha tree. The light of earthen lamp played across her features. As soon as Jyestha saw Lakshmi, a desire arose in Jyestha's heart. The desire to win everything that she could from Lakshmi on this night. The two sisters had beheld each other after years.

Jyestha recalled how Lakshmi had made her carry her down the mountain to the trader's house and whatever had happened after it. A dubious smile was plastered on her face. With the same mantra that Kali had taught her, Jyestha manifested the dice board between herself and Lakshmi.

"*Anujaa*, shall we play? You know it is customary to play dice on this night of Deepavali. Shouldn't we play as sisters?" Jyestha slipped on the role of a caring older sister with finesse. Lakshmi's brown eyes expanded with surprise and affection. She chuckled. Her sister's fingers traced the contours of the dice board. Jyestha waited.

"*Agrajaa*, I thought you would never ask. Let us play without any stake."

Jyestha nodded. No stakes were required among family members as it could lead to unnecessary discord. She allowed Lakshmi to arrange the pawns on the board. A light wind rustled the leaves of the Asvattha tree. Its heart-shaped leaves revolved.

"But *Anujaa*, I have a request, the loser of all three rounds can request any two boons from the winner. I shall only play if you agree to this request." Jyestha's throat was heavy with emotion. "After all, we have met after so long."

Lakshmi agreed. She shuffled the dice and made her first move. Jyestha watched every throw, scrutinizing Lakshmi's skill level. She resisted the urge to smirk. Their ornaments tinkled as they played, uttering exclamations and sighs as the rounds progressed. Her sister was such a poor player, despite being the goddess of wealth. Jyestha pitied her, and it was easier to play worse and lose on purpose. The most important rule that Kali had taught her was to feign every emotion in front of an opponent. Let them think that they have won and strike at an opportune moment, to grab something far more substantial.

"Ah, *agrajaa*, It seems I have won." Lakshmi murmured, her face was red with shame. "It does not suit the younger sister to grant the elder any boons, but I will not go back on my word. You gave me immense joy by initiating this game."

Your joy will turn to tears soon, anujaa.

"For the first boon, I would ask that my lord husband Kali become a Yuga Purusha. For the second boon, I implore that the Trimurti shall not interfere in his ruling when Kali assumes power. That's all I ask, *kanistha*."

Lakshmi's face paled. Her pink lips trembled, parting in shock. The realisation made her features crumble satisfyingly. Jyestha's face remained stony, except for a subtle smirk. Lakshmi averted her eyes. Then in a low voice she uttered,

"*Tathastu*. So be it."

Jyestha stared at the dice board and then at the line on her right palm.

If I have to make my fortune by deception, I will stop at nothing to get where I should be. With this...our fates are sealed.

7.

Kali Yuga

The two boons spelled disaster in the realm of the Devas and the Asuras. The Devas were stunned. The Asuras were looking for a new opportunity. The humans remained oblivious as ever to the on-going tension between Devaloka and Patalaloka. Kali's position as a Yuga Purusha granted him immense power. Jyestha's second boon stung like the bite of a vicious serpent in the hearts of all.

In the midst of this tension, Kali's new capital, Vishashan prospered. Located in *Mrityuloka*, Kali poured his heart and soul into his empire. The Asvattha tree became an important landmark of Vishashan. Kali had an ostentatious plan for everything. The funds came from the wealth Jyestha and Kali had won through deception and cheating. Jyestha assumed her new role as a queen like a fish to water.

Though Kali's reign would be the shortest of the epochs, 1200 divine years, his might remained uncontested thanks to Lakshmi's blessing. Kali's dark power, the secret one which could corrupt and manipulate the hearts of humans and force them to make mistakes, trapped everyone in its net. Kali fooled a human King called Nala and deprived him of his wealth and kingdom. That became the foundation of his ascension to power.

Kali and Jyestha changed. The bond between them, that had tightened like a yoke, began to fray. Kali remained immersed in statecraft, outlining and expanding his empire. Jyestha realised then, that the Gandharva harboured greed for power. The great-grandson of Adharma and Mithya had been waiting beyond the curtain-hall to take the centre stage. Kali had built up this dream of a great play with himself as the central character, Jyestha had listened to it countless times and approved of his ambition but the vices that came along with the blessing of a kingdom and his powerful connections were something that Jyestha could not condone.

Kali drank, gambled and charmed human women. Jyestha bewildered by the changing behaviour of her lord, drew away from him and threw herself into her duties of a queen, pretending that it did not bother her that he had other consorts. Once the pair that had traversed *Mrityuloka* with linked arms, stayed in different parts of Vishashan's grand palace. The luxuries and the satisfaction of being a '*raja-patni*' diminished. Ruling a kingdom was a difficult task, and Jyestha noticed that Kali began neglecting his duties, preferring to shut himself up with his cronies like Gandharva Dvapara and gambling his nights away.

For Jyestha herself, nothing changed. She remained devout to Mahadeva and fulfilled her responsibilities. When she stared out of the palace window at the intricate gardens and the sprawling city streets she felt as though she sorely lacked something important. She was still an accomplished actress, the Devi of misfortune that built her husband's fortune through deception. The Devas and Asuras feared her even more. But did they respect her? Did Lakshmi respect her? All Jyestha wanted at this point, was to step into Vaikuntha with her head held with pride.

Due to Kali's actions however, Jyestha would not merit respect. The Gandharva had become too arrogant for his own well-being and now, when he had previously prized her opinion and been eager to teach her, he began to dismiss her and ignore her. Jyestha hated being ignored. It reminded of the unpleasant times in *Mrityuloka* during her abandonment.

Why can I not be happy? What does Lakshmi have that I do not and even though I have everything I have ever wanted, why am I so discontent?

One fine afternoon, Kali knocked on the door of her bed-chamber. Jyestha who had been resting in the afternoon, opened the door, surprised to see her lord at the threshold. She invited him in. Kali fiddled with his royal silk robes and stumbled in until he was properly seated on the cushioned platform that the entertainers often occupied.

Even after becoming a King, he has not forgotten his status as a Gandharva?

"*Priye*, I have great news." Kali's blue eyes were blazing with excitement. Jyestha adjusted the drape of her silk sari and sat at a respectful distance from him. She prepared the betel-leaf as customary and presented it to him with a stoic expression. These days, his mood was unpredictable, Kali would be buoyant and indulgent one moment, wrathful and venomous the next, silent and uncooperative at other times. Jyestha held her breath, waiting to assess which mood he might display.

"Asura Virochana's penance is over. He managed to solicit a great boon from Lord Surya. A glittering diadem, one that renders the wearer invincible. And guess who he is coming to see?" Jyestha's eyes widened in surprise. Kali's smug smile played on his flushed arrogant face.

"Who?" She asked with awe, as though she wasn't clever enough to guess.

"Me." Kali presented the official letter to her with a flourish. Jyestha took the parchment and read it. Her eyebrows furrowed slightly on reading the scroll. Virochana already spoke about Kali as a great friend and was praising his might in the letter. It made

Jyestha uneasy. Flattery was a tool that the opponents often used to win an ally's trust. How could Kali possibly fall for this?

"He wants an alliance with us to wage a war against the Devas." Jyestha spoke aloud. Kali straightened, pressing his back into the wall. He raised a single eyebrow at the tone of distress in her voice. Jyestha realised she was openly frowning.

"*Priye*, tell me, why am I doing all this? Can you not display a slight happiness at this great task I have managed to accomplish? Asura Virochana, whose capital in Patalaloka I visited as an entertainer is coming to see me as an equal. Do you realise that between the two of us we can conquer Vaikuntha in one fell swoop? Your dream, Jyestha is about to be realised!" Kali's powerful fingers were digging into her arms as he shook her, like he wanted her to wake from a dream and snap into reality. His expression was one of glee. Jyestha winced.

"My lord...you're hurting me." She murmured. Her husband sighed, releasing his hold. Jyestha scooted to a side, rubbing the place where her flesh stung. Sometimes Kali did not know his own strength.

"I am sorry. I should not have acted like that." Jyestha fixed her eyes onto the chequered marbled floor which soured Kali's mood. "How many times should I tell you, look at me when you speak. I have told you time and time again, that you should never bow your head, *priye*." Kali's expression was stern as he scowled. He gripped her chin forcing her gaze back to his face.

"What is your opinion?" The softness in his voice made her heart skip a beat. When her husband spoke like that, Jyestha knew he was trying to read her thoughts and make her reveal her weaknesses. There was always this tension between them as the Yuga progressed and his power as a Yuga Purusha grew. Once he had told her that he prized her opinion.

These days he preferred flatters who stoked his ego. A master of deception was falling for the wiles that he employed, and Kali wasn't even aware that he had become so easy to manipulate. Jyestha had discerned the truth due to her intelligence. It was this truth that she shared as counsel.

"My lord, I shall only ask you to proceed with caution. You once told me that Asuras are masters of deception and *maya*. You are the newly elected Yuga Purusha and Lakshmi's boons ensure that the Trimurti shall not interfere in your rule. Asura Virochana might take advantage of this."

"I see." Kali looked away. His eyes were fixed on the sun that was dipping westward. Jyestha's chamber was bathed in sunlight. It reminded of the moment that she had first met Kali in the forest, on the banks of the river Pushpabhadra. His expression was unreadable for an instant before he scoffed.

"You see, that's exactly the opposite of what my ministers told me. Dvapara and everyone else insisted that we arrange a game of dice to welcome Virochana and forge an alliance. You have been spending too much time with fear mongers like Vrinda and Malati. I only brought the devakanya's as your companions to the palace because you were so lonely. But I see you have been swayed by their gossip." Jyestha heaved a sigh. Kali never spared them any insult. She knew why and her temper rose.

"You hate them because they rejected you. Vrinda and Malati are my friends. Please stop insulting them." Jyestha's tone grew sharp. It was the wrong thing to say. Kali's eyes narrowed. As the argument between them escalated and they hurled vile insults at each other, Jyestha's handmaidens and guards eavesdropped. Quite soon the palace would be rife with true gossip. That the king and his *patni* were at loggerheads. Jyestha hated the fact that no one respected their privacy.

Every word she said only stoked the fire of Kali's ire until he hurled one of the decanters of wine right into the mirror and left her to clean the mess.

"You truly are Alakshmi, the goddess of misfortune!" Kali barreled out of her chambers with this parting shot. It shattered Jyestha's heart, who was only looking out for her lord. Kali had been her teacher and her support in the most trying time of her life. To hear him say the words that the world had whispered at her emergence meant she was losing him to his own forces of darkness. Why did it turn out like this?

The tears that streamed down her cheeks as she knelt and wept bounced off the palace walls. But Jyestha wasn't weeping because Kali had insulted her, she was weeping at the folly of her younger self that had married Dussaha.

When the Trimurti did not stand up for me, why did I not stand up for myself?

A few weeks later Virochana and Kali forged an alliance. Jyestha was not allowed to witness it. Ironic as it was, women were not allowed in dice halls. Kali's distrust of her and his insecurity that she once wanted to influence Virochana made him lock her up in the palace. Jyestha stared at her reflection in the broken mirror, refusing to replace it. She was oiling and braiding her hair with a blank expression her her face. Jyestha stared at the tiny container of kumkum, wondering if she should adorn it or not.

What an inauspicious thought. Kali may have changed, but I do not want him to suffer any misfortune. My circumstances are quite ironic. I wanted to be the villain of this stage-play, but even that role was stolen from me. Mahadeva, what is the merit of my devotion to you?

"Jyestha."

Jyestha stirred from her reverie. In the distorted reflection, she saw Vrinda and Malati. "What news have you brought?" Jyestha asked the pair of devakanyas. "No news, Devi, however, a *tapasvini* who wishes to see you. We tried to send her away, but she was quite persistent." Vrinda whispered. The two devakanyas harboured a sense of guilt, because they got wind of Jyestha and Kali's argument. The whole palace was buzzing with gossip.

"We must never send *tapasvinis* away, invite her inside."

When the old woman was shown in, Jyestha recognised her instantly. She dismissed her companions and the guards, shutting the door of her chambers to ensure privacy. The *tapasvini* sat cross-legged on the pedestal, a brass kamandalu at her side. Her ochre robes looked out of place in the opulence of the room. The scent of blue lotuses wafted in the air mingling with the scent of burning sandalwood which were used to purify the air in Jyestha's chambers.

"*Agrajaa.* I gave you everything you asked for." Lakshmi spoke through clenched teeth. Jyestha sat straighter as she stared at her sisters livid expression in the broken mirror. Lakshmi's disguise faded and she revealed her true self. Jyestha ran her fingers over her thick braid, which she began coiling into a bun. After it she leaned towards her reflection, carefully dabbing the *sindura* in the parting of her hair. There were dark circles around her eyes and her complexion appeared lusterless despite her makeup.

"Did you? You made the most vital decision of my life, the decision where I was entitled to my choice. The decision of my marriage. Did I have no right to choose my lord?" Jyestha's coppery eyes blazed as she countered. She reminded herself that she should speak tactfully. She beheld Lakshmi's face, which resembled a wilted lotus. So her sister was suffering too? Good.

"Who would you have chosen, Jyestha? Virochana? Indra? You chose Kali, and where did it get you? Do you know how many innocent lives will perish in this war? You can prevent it!" Lakshmi's voice resounded like a clap of thunder as she shifted on the mat. Jyestha's patience was shattering under its assault. She fidgeted on the golden pedestal attempting to reign in her temper. Lakshmi's words hurt like a bed of thorns in *Mrityuloka's* forests.

"Why is it my responsibility in the first place? Kali is beyond reason, he does not care about a single word I say. Are you forgetting that my brother-in-law and Narada Muni had a hand in my marriage to Kali? Or are you going to ignore that? Why do the Trimurti remain silent in matters of chaos? They have greater influence than you or me." Jyestha whirled to face Lakshmi, her remark stung the air. Lakshmi's serene face darkened.

"Because of you. If you hadn't asked for those boons—"

"Because of me? How convenient. The Trimurti will witness all the chaos in the three worlds and find a single woman to blame, *Alakshmi* the Devi of misfortune, whose very steps lead to discord. Tell me, *anujaa*, why is it always a woman who is to blame for the chaos that occurs in the universe? Why is Ahalya punished for Indra's sins and why should I be held responsible for Kali's?"

Jyestha's question inflamed Lakshmi's face as though the goddess had been slapped. Her sisters gaze did not waver but the humiliation in her expression was evident.

Anasuya and Arundathi were prized for enriching the glory of their lord, while Diti and Aditi, Vinita and Kadru were held responsible for the problems between the Devas and Asuras and the Nagas and Garuda. However, the greed that churns in the hearts of men like a deadly poison is never blamed. The perception of those that populate this Brahmanda always finds a woman to blame for its misfortune. Lakshmi can never understand it.

"*Agrajaa*, you can punish me, you can unleash your wrath upon me, but please, do not unleash this terror onto the three worlds. Only you have the power to bring Kali back to his senses, as a wife that is your dharma." Lakshmi murmured softly.

That was the worst thing her sister could have said at this moment.

Jyestha's face grew cold and devoid of any pity. She grabbed the kamandalu that rested beside Lakshmi and emptied the potent water onto her head with a curse. The water dripped down her sister's head who gasped in shock.

"I curse you to descend into Patala. I never want to see your face again, Lakshmi."

The kamandalu clattered onto the floor with a loud clang. Jyestha hissed like a venomous serpent and Lakshmi gasped. A moment later she vanished from the chamber as though she had evaporated into thin air. The silence that lingered in the empty space resembled a death knell. Jyestha swallowed, a chill went up her spine.

"What have I become?" Jyestha felt suddenly anxious and frightened by her own action.

8.

The Loka of Illusions

The sky was a pale ivory. Against this backdrop, small fires burned, giving off the stench of smoke and flesh. People lamented and cried. The ground was blackened, cracked and hard. Jyestha walked barefoot, unable to the sense the thorns and stones that pricked her soles. Her feet were caked in soot, and she left a trail in the ashy precinct of the cremation ground. Vishashan had charred to ash and the cries of its subjects rent the atmosphere. Jyestha could not bring herself to shed a single tear. Clad in a white sari she sat unblinking in the cremation ground like a ghost.

Her fears had not been unfounded.

Virochana had betrayed Kali. Her lord husband had not heeded her warning and *Mrityuloka* had paid the price for it. The almighty Asura had pretended to befriend Kali and had promised him Vaikuntha. He had assured Kali that he would let him have the dominion of *Mrityuloka* and that while Virochana ruled Devaloka Kali would rule Vaikuntha. Kali had been too blind and too arrogant to glimpse the Asura's deceit. For all his accomplishments of a political scholar, her husband was a victim of his own weaknesses, and his advisors were useless. They changed sides like cowards when Kali landed the losing throw and joined Virochana instead.

With the empowering coronet of Surya Deva that granted Virochana invincibility the Devas were imprisoned. Virochana installed himself as the King of the three worlds by right of conquest and ascended Indra's throne. Jyestha and Kali were in a bind for due to Lakshmi's boon to Jyestha, that the Trimurti would not interfere in Kali's rule. And if the Trimurti could not interfere, the Asuras would rule the three worlds forever. Kali and Jyestha had figuratively fallen to their deaths while chasing the brilliant chariot of the sun and they realised their powerlessness.

The first blow that Virochana dealt them was the dismantling of their empire. Kali's other consorts scattered like frightened doves to avoid being taken as a prize by the Asura army. Jyestha did not blame them. Kali and Jyestha were now homeless, forced into exile as they witnessed the horror their actions had inflicted on innocents. Virochana banned the worship of the Devas and established himself as the only one worthy of worship. His asuras tormented anyone who dared to defy his rules. As their city burned and their subjects cried for mercy, Kali and Jyestha fled like cowards.

Agrajaa, I would take your misfortune upon my head if you allowed me. Please do not walk down this path of destruction. You shall regret it.

Lakshmi's words echoed in Jyestha's head. She understood then, what her sister had meant and now it was too late to regret. Jyestha understood what she had been lacking as she sat caked in ashes. She had lacked *karuna*. Jyestha had lived and thought only about herself and her goals, ignoring the discomfort she had caused to her sister. She had failed to counsel Kali and steer him onto a better path.

The wrong sister went to Patala. It should have been me. I wish I could beg her forgiveness.

The sole reason why Virochana was further empowered was due to Lakshmi's presence in Patala. Jyestha's curse spelt disaster for the Devas, but even Jyestha found no malicious glee could mitigate the depth of her guilt and sorrow. Without Lakshmi, Lord Vishnu would not act. Without *Shri*, Indra could not restore himself to power. Without Lakshmi, there was no compassion, purity or mercy. Jyestha's malevolent influence brought out the worst in Devas, Asuras and men. She had single-handedly toppled the order in the three worlds, but the most astounding fact was she could not restore it to its original shape.

Jyestha's lower lip trembled, and she finally broke into a loud wail. Her body was wracked with guilt and repentance. Jyestha cried and the world fell silent to finally listen to the cry of the goddess that it had neglected. The goddess that craved respect. Jyestha did not want to be feared. She wanted to be loved and adored, to not feel as though she was a burden that had to be borne or tolerated. Jyestha felt Kali's gentle touch on her head.

"*Priye.* Forgive me. I was a fool." Kali's tone was contrite. The touch of his fingers on her head was the most soothing and caring he had been in the past few years. Jyestha's head remained bowed in fear.

"My lord must abandon me as well." She murmured. "Run away, you will suffer if you stay with me."

"Jyestha." He put his arms around her and held her still. As Jyestha sobbed, he soothed her. In the middle of the cremation ground, they made a wretched pair, led astray by their vices and shortsightedness. Jyestha only wished that he would turn his back on her and retreat so that she could atone for her sins. She did not deserve any comfort or pity when she could not extend the same.

"I shall never abandon you." Kali asserted. "When I possessed the human king Nala and caused him to lose his kingdom, he and his wife Damayanti were forced into exile. To torment Nala further I influenced him to abandon his sleeping wife in the forest." Jyestha's eyes widened with shock. She had not known this story. A shiver crept up her spine. Jyestha was acutely familiar with Damayanti's distress. Kali's eyes glistened with remorse. The air between them shimmered due to the acrid smoke.

"The pain that Damayanti went through because of my action is something I would never wish on you, *priye.* Perhaps, I was fated to lose this kingdom due to my deceit, my wrath and my envy over being rejected by the princess at her Swayamvar. Jyestha, you must not blame yourself for my sins." Kali's hand dropped onto her shoulder, and he squeezed it softly. Jyestha could hardly process the secrets that he held close to his chest, like a Naga that coiled itself around its precious possessions.

"I failed you." Kali continued in a sombre tone. His throat was choked with emotion. "I only...Jyestha when you emerged from the poison of the Naga Vasuki, I believed that this was the Devi that I wanted by my side, as my wife. You were a vision as you appeared like a flame, with your head held high. However, I felt unworthy of you. When Sage Dussaha accepted your hand, I was jealous. Driven by that jealousy, I did something unthinkable."

Jyestha raised her puffy face upward, wilted and bathed in tears as it was. Kali had never spoken about this before. He had desired her? She was desirable in his eyes? Kali's words were changing her perception of herself. She had believed that he had seduced her due to his ambition and that his words were lies. That she had fallen in a trap like an abandoned woman who had no other option but to accept any man that bestowed her some affection to survive in *Mrityuloka.*

"What did you do?" Her question sounded sterner than she had intended.

"...I spread rumors in Devaloka about your negative influence. I had seen you once or twice at the banks of the Sarasvati at night and it was easy to tell some crazy stories. I...honestly I deserve all this punishment because it was my words that led Sage Dussaha to consult Rishi Markandeya about your character. I had no idea that my behaviour would lead to your abandonment. I foolishly thought, I could restore your identity and the damage I had done."

Kali's face was red with shame and guilt. Her lord could not meet Jyestha's fierce glare. Her palm itched and for the first and the last time in her life she dealt him a resounding smack, right across his unblemished cheek. Jyestha drew her hand back and clenched her fist as though to control her emotions.

"You are a liar. You are vile. A coward! Did you think if you approached me, I would reject you? Why didn't you speak up in Vaikuntha when Lakshmi asked who would have my hand?"

"*Priye*, what are you saying—"

"I suffered endlessly due to your mistakes, your pride, ego and vanity. I hurt my sister who wished for my prosperity for your sake! For your glory, so that you would stop giving yourself false airs, have a fixed station and not feel sorry for yourself! All of this would have been resolved or might have never occurred if you had not been a fool and had told me that you loved me!" Jyestha's voice cracked like lightning and her expression was one of exasperation and wrath. She appeared fearsome with her hair unbound and her form shimmering like a dark flame.

"...*priye*. You are not angry because I tarnished your image? I think you are missing the point here." Kali spoke anxiously. He was crouched in front of her with an expression of awe and fear. His eyes burned blue, his lips were parted. He appeared like fallen tree. Jyestha for a moment marveled at how her presence frightened him.

"My image was sculpted the moment Lord Brahma proclaimed I was Alakshmi. In the end, whether you actively ruined my reputation or not, people would have still feared me or may have been wary of me. You only added a crazy twist to my narrative with your lies." Jyestha scowled. Kali remained silent. His gaze was still on her feet. Finally, he touched her soles in reverence.

"Devi, your heart is a sea of compassion. Someone like me, does not deserve this leniency." Jyestha sighed. She raised an eyebrow, recalling those dramas Vrinda and Malati liked to enact. The ones where the women fell to their husbands' feet and wept for forgiveness.

"You aren't going to weep and beg for mercy?" Jyestha asked lightly, her irritation fading. Having Kali bow to her in this way appeased her ire. Kali raised his eyes, and his face was crimson. It was the first time Jyestha had seen her husband blush. "Devi, I have a man's pride."

"Your pride led to this complication in the first place. I won't forgive you unless you make it dramatic." She heard him laugh softly and then Kali did as she asked. He begged for forgiveness till his voice was hoarse and Jyestha could not hold back her laughter and she forgave him. She forgave him because it was plain to see his actions had been of a fool in love.

"I must go to Patala. Alone. Only I can locate Lakshmi and restore the order in the three realms. I hope she shall forgive me and I will convince her to take back the two boons. The longer Virochana reigns, the more our subjects will suffer. I will find a way to bring him down." Jyestha's tone was determined.

The two left the cremation grounds to the Asvattha tree, where Jyestha had been abandoned. The most important landmark in Vishashan. The tree had grown and spread its myriad branches. The heart shaped leaves revolved in the still air. Jyestha placed a hand across the bark. Kali had discovered that the secret tunnels that lead to the mysterious realm of the Asuras and Nagas that could be accessed only through certain portals, ran right under the roots of this tree.

Jyestha harnessed her powers and felt the inexorable magic link her to Patala. As the offspring of Naga Vasuki, who co-ruled the Patala with Asura Virochana, Jyestha found she could access this realm. When Kali and her had been scheming to infiltrate into Virochana's domain in their early days, they had planned to use this portal. Jyestha felt the solid structure of *Mrityuloka* ebb away as she descended. The pathways of Patalaloka often shifted so that intruders lost their way.

Jyestha kept her eyes wide open as she walked. She could not use an *arani* to light her way for the Nagas hated fire. Any sign of smoke would cause them to turn into enemies. The subterranean realm shimmered and shifted. At times her path was lit by the faint light of the treasure hoarded by the Nagas. Some of it was illusion, some of it was real but it would curse the ones who dared to steal it. The semblance of ground shaped itself across her soles. The paths were wet and slimy like the skin of a giant serpent. Swallowing her revulsion and keeping her fear at bay, Jyestha charted her path.

Around her the air buzzed with hisses and whispers. The apparitions of the spirits trapped in Patala often lured those that dared to enter. They whispered deceptions in one's ear and the illusions of the Asura cities rippled in the nebulous domain. Those that entered those cities never returned, for the luxuries there were so lavish that they bewitched those with greed. Jyestha only thought of Lakshmi due to which she was able to identify the path that the goddess had taken. Jyestha ventured deeper into the heart of Patala where there was complete absence of light. The faint luminescence of Lakshmi's footsteps burned brightly in the darkness guiding her path.

No matter how the fear and the whispers sought to tempt her, Jyestha walked on, her heart fixed on Lakshmi. How had Lakshmi made the journey? Her younger sister was used to the brilliance and splendour of Vaikuntha, Jyestha knew that Lakshmi did not like Patala.

I failed to do my dharma as an older sister which is to protect her. If I truly deserve forgiveness, I shall reach her under any circumstances. Otherwise, I shall never resurface from this realm.

The darkness deepened and it enveloped her like a funeral shroud. Jyestha strengthens her resolve. Her eyes expanded as she glimpsed a bright light. Was this opening where Lakshmi had gone? However, the light was coming her way. It neared like an ivory flame. Jyestha's steps faltered and she came to a standstill.

"...Dussaha?"

The name of her former husband left her lips. Jyestha's face whitened. Dussaha stood before her examining her closely as though he did not recognise her at all. He had not aged. His white beard shone in the darkness, as did his garments, however Jyestha could not discern his form.

"Please do not stand in my way, my lord." Jyestha requested.

The figure of Dussaha did not stir. He stood like an impenetrable mountain that blocked her route to Lakshmi. Jyestha waited until she felt the irritation rise.

"I asked you to move out of my way." Jyestha did not wish to be impolite, however she felt a myriad of conflicting emotions. The sight of her former husband was something she had never felt she would see. Their paths had diverged, and Jyestha felt, it should have stayed that way. Was he back to torment and taunt her?

"Why did you do it, my lord?" Jyestha finally uttered, seething with rage. "Why did you abandon me? You could have told me you had a problem with me, and I would have left. Your action caused me unnecessary torment and I lost my true nature. I became a *kritya*, a monster because you created a monster of me in your head. You wished to tame me, but you couldn't handle my power, now you roam here like an evil spirit, and you try to block my way! Are you not done?"

When Jyestha screamed, the figure of Dussaha rippled and spoke in a disembodied voice.

"It is true Jyestha. I have been reduced to this because I abandoned someone I was supposed to protect. From a sage, I have become a ghoul. The only thing that can release me is your forgiveness. Otherwise, I shall roam here for an eternity."

Jyestha felt disgust and pity at Dussaha's current form. She averted her eyes and spoke in low broken voice, "Go my lord. I forgive you, do not haunt this realm of the Nagas." It came easily to her, and Jyestha's heart lightened when the apparition vanished. She felt as though a great burden had been washed off her shoulders. As soon as the words fell from her lips, the darkness surrounding Jyestha was uplifted, as though a veil had been cast away.

"What is..." The sky was suddenly a brilliant blue and Jyestha could hear the roar of a great ocean. She stared, entranced as though she had witnessed the greatest magic trick. Whoever had cast it was truly the master of illusion.

Blinking rapidly so that she could adjust to the light, Jyestha's mouth fell open.

"Daughter." Naga Vasuki in his humanoid form stepped forward to receive her. Her father's silver eyes gleamed with affection. Jyestha knelt to touch his feet and accept his blessings. She understood that she had been tested. Raising her head so that it was proud and straight, Jyestha uttered.

"Take me to Lakshmi."

9.

Alakshmi's Deception

Lakshmi's brown eyes bore into Jyestha as she knelt before her sister. Today Jyestha realised why they were twins. Their appearances were different, but they did not differ in attitudes. Lakshmi being younger needed to be persuaded more. Her anger once aroused was far deadlier than Jyestha's short temperament. Lakshmi could hold onto a grudge tenaciously if she wished.

The sound of the ocean in the palace of the Asura Varuna, Lakshmi's adopted father was constant. It did not allow them to speak in whispers. The scintillating white crystal palace was more ethereal than any *sabha* in the three worlds, Lakshmi sat like a queen. Perhaps her sister was just being haughty. Jyestha sighed, discerning her childishness.

"*Anujaa*, I apologised a hundred times." Jyestha whined. Lakshmi crossed her dainty feet, pointedly turning her head the other way. She still wore the garb of a *tapasvini* and had braided her lustrous locks into a single braid like a woman who had taken an oath. Varuna and Vasuki, two males far removed from the temperament of women shifted uneasily. They stood at a distance. Jyestha reached for Lakshmi's feet again.

"No. Do not touch my feet."

Jyestha sighed. She remained kneeling and desperate for any

positive reaction. Her sister's pretty lips remained pouted and sullen. Jyestha wondered if she should now start extolling her beauty or appeal to the compassion within her heart.

"Why are you here?" Lakshmi asked, addressing not Jyestha but the blade of kusha grass. Jyestha was now despondent. If Lakshmi would not forgive her and come back, the order in the three worlds would remain chaotic.

"Please revoke the two boons that you gave me." Jyestha pleaded.

"You won't care if your lord husband is removed from his post as Yuga Purusha?" Lakshmi asked. She did not believe Jyestha. Jyestha knew Kali would object but she had to persuade Lakshmi under any circumstances. The longer she stayed, the more dire the situation for the Devas. Jyestha swallowed her pride.

"Kali shall not mind it."

"That's a lie." Lakshmi shifted and for a moment Jyestha wondered if her sister was only play acting. If not, she pitied her brother-in-law, Vishnu. Who knew Lakshmi was capable of throwing such a tantrum? Was it like this in every situation?

"Consider my request. If you do not take back the boons, Virochana will only grow more ruthless, and the three worlds shall collapse." Jyestha reasoned.

"I suppose you will not question why I cannot trust you. You wanted Virochana to destroy the Devas and he is doing just that. Why do you have a change of heart?" Lakshmi now gazed at Jyestha in a calculating manner. Jyestha felt intimidated and annoyed.

"Because I realised my mistake. I should have understood your point of view. If I had counseled Kali properly, Virochana might have never risen to power. *Anujaa*, I accept that I was driven by envy and malice, and I wished to destroy the happiness you owned, because I had not found mine. I was discontent with what fate had dealt to me and I held you responsible because..." Jyestha trailed away. Her words were weighted by emotion.

"Because?"

"Because you are my sister. My only family. I hoped then that you would understand the torment in my heart and understand why I felt rejected. I wanted you to stand up for me and stand by my side." Jyestha realised that this was what she had wanted all along.

"So then, will you stand up for me and stand by my side? I have not put you on a trial, *Agrajaa.*" Lakshmi's soft utterance was like a soothing balm to the wounds of her heart. Jyestha's eyes widened. Then she pursed her lips, imitating Lakshmi's pout.

"Since when did you learn how to manipulate people?" Jyestha glowered. Lakshmi snickered. Her sister took her hand, in friendship and in sisterhood. Lakshmi's palm was soft, her smile was wide and entrancing. Jyestha knew she had been forgiven and breathed a huge sigh of relief. Vasuki and Varuna matched Jyestha's sigh.

"I revoke the power of the two boons given to Jyestha." Lakshmi uttered. Jyestha sensed the invisible ripple of magic that snapped into two like broken bow-string once Lakshmi uttered those words.

"Daughter, you must return to Vaikuntha and take your rightful seat next to your lord." Varuna murmured. Lakshmi glanced at her father and shook her head.

"My reappearance in Vaikuntha will alert Virochana. We should let him believe that I am still imprisoned in Patala and cannot ascend. If he suspects the slightest threat to his power, he might be provoked into action." Lakshmi paced in the chamber. Jyestha followed her figure, studying her mannerisms. This was the first time that Jyestha was studying Lakshmi closely. The lessons that Kali had taught her about studying people to refine her skills lingered in her mind.

"I have to agree with you." Jyestha murmured. She noted

Lakshmi's gait, her posture, the gleam in her eyes, the way she fidgeted. Jyestha's mind had already devised a plan, but she hesitated. Would her sister agree to go along with it? Noting Jyestha's intense concentration on her activities Lakshmi threw her a puzzled glance.

"*Agrajaa*, do not tell me you are cooking up some grandiose scheme."

Jyestha tittered, impressed by how Lakshmi had read her mind.

"I am. This scheme is not without peril but falls within my expertise. You shall not undertake any risk. As your older sister, I must do my best to protect you." Jyestha rose and, in a trice, she transformed herself into Lakshmi. Lakshmi's eyes went so wide, Jyestha was afraid that they would start from her sockets. Even Vasuki and Varuna were alarmed.

Jyestha circled around Lakshmi taking her hand and exchanging places a couple of times to confound her audience. Varuna and Vasuki watched bemused until Jyestha paused. In the perfect imitation of Lakshmi's sweet voice, Jyestha asked, "Can you guess who is the real Lakshmi?"

Vasuki and Varuna were speechless. Jyestha matched Lakshmi's every expression which made it impossible for them to detect the deception. Just as they were about to announce their decision, Jyestha heard the strum of the veena.

"*Narayan, Narayan.* Devi, I have been sent—" Narada Muni who had made his appearance stood dumbfounded at the manifestation of two Lakshmi's. He glanced from Varuna to Vasuki and beheld the sisters cautiously.

"What is the meaning of this?"

Jyestha was about to speak but Lakshmi interrupted her.

"Ah, *devarishi*, can you tell which one of us is the real Lakshmi? After all, you are all-knowing." Jyestha snickered inwardly. This was the perfect opportunity to get back at Rishi Narada and she was glad her sister was supporting her. Jyestha noticed how Narada observed them. He had to do it from a distance, and she watched his expression turn from indulgent to panicky.

"I..I cannot guess..." Narada murmured humbly. A moment later he cleared his throat. "I stand defeated Devi, I cannot tell apart my real mistress from the false one." He joined his palms in defeat. Jyestha dissolved the illusion, her face beaming with triumph.

"If the devarishi is fooled, there is no reason Virochana shall not fall for it. I bear a strong grudge against him for cheating my lord husband, so I shall use my power to bring him down." Jyestha's eyes gleamed with malice. Lakshmi's lips parted in a soft gasp.

"As far as I know, Virochana remains undefeated as long as he has his crown. Virochana is also quite fond of playing dice games. When Kali hosted him at Vishashan they played almost every night. I shall play with Lakshmi as a stake."

The declaration brought a string of protests from the three men. However, Lakshmi was staring at Jyestha fixedly, with a hint of pride. She stepped forward and grasped Jyestha's hand tightly.

"I bless you with good fortune, Jyestha. Return victorious to Vaikuntha."

Jyestha nodded. Then between Narada, Varuna and Vasuki they discussed the intricacies of the plan and refined it until it was flawless. Jyestha would approach Virochana in disguise and keep him occupied while Narada escorted the real Lakshmi back to Vaikuntha. The fact that it was the eve of Deepavali was not lost to Jyestha. Virochana would be relaxed, his Asuras would be languorous and eager to play.

Jyestha transformed into Lakshmi and arrived at Devaloka. The palace of Indra and the cities of Devaloka were decorated with many thousand lamps. The entire city was festooned with sweet smelling garlands and the pathways were painted with auspicious designs. Devaloka rose as a vision of grandeur and its light scintillated in the waters of the Sarasvati. Jyestha entered, invisible and undeterred. She stepped past the carpeted hallways and ascended the marbled steps to the gambling chamber. Jyestha heard the sounds of laughter inside the dice hall. She quickly revealed herself, putting an end to the laughter.

The Asuras whispered as Jyestha stepped towards Virochana, who was seated on a cushioned platform his eyes affixed to the dice board. Virochana was stately, his swarthy features exuded a shrewdness that Kali had not foreseen. He was dressed richly, and his crimson irises dilated as he noticed Jyestha.

"Devi. What brings you to my humble abode?" Virochana was polite as he invited Jyestha to take a seat. Jyestha sat. The other Asuras were gathered around, their curiosity growing. The sight of a Devi in the dice hall was unheard of in the other realms.

"I wander the three realms to bless my devotees. You too are my devotee. You were dissatisfied with Lord Indra for he tricked you into losing your fortune. However, you are punishing the three realms for it." Jyestha's tone was measured and calm. Virochana's eyelids flickered, waiting for Jyestha to continue.

"I am deeply pained by the condition of my devotees, so I put forth a proposal that may require your consideration. Asura king, the one who possesses *Shri* attains felicity and becomes renowned in the three worlds. Today you play this game to ensure your good fortune, but you shall not want for it if I remain by your side."

The assembly of Asuras burst into laughter. Some faces were awed, others incredulous. Virochana silenced the gathering with a single glance. Jyestha glanced at the crown that glittered on his royal head.

"Devi, this proposal is absurd. You are ever devoted to Lord Vishnu. Why would you suddenly desert your lord and come to me?

I cannot believe you." Virochana's expression was bemused.

"You misunderstand. What I mean is I wish to play a game of dice with you with myself as a stake. If you win, I shall desert the Devas and remain in Patala forever for your well-being. If you lose, you shall have to give me whatever I ask for. Tell me great Asura, do you accept my proposal?" Jyestha's voice resounded in the gambling chamber, silencing everyone. It was her greatest moment of power, having a room full powerful beings silenced by her very words. Jyestha knew that Virochana could not back down. A woman had challenged him and if he forfeited, it would damage his pride as the King of the Asuras.

Virochana, already quite assured of his might in a dice game and enticed with the possibility of having the Devi stationed in Patala, which meant Lakshmi would always favour him, assented immediately ignoring the wise words of his advisors. The game began and Alakshmi's fortune wrecked its havoc on Virochana who was blinded by arrogance and had underestimated Jyestha.

As the game progressed, it was pure joy to watch the oppositions expression crumble and grow increasingly panicked at the impending defeat. Jyestha put everything Kali had taught her into practice, wishing her lord was here to witness her success. Jyestha prolonged the game, interspersing with well-timed anecdotes that kept the Asuras engrossed. Lakshmi had to reach Vaikuntha safely.

At the last roll of the dice, Jyestha sat back in her seat, regal and queenly, imbued with divine power. The sheer joy on her face shimmered through her disguise.

"It seems you have lost. I hope you shall not go back on your word." Jyestha murmured calmly.

"I am an Asura King. I never would break my word to a Devi." Virochana's tone was subdued, although she could plainly witness his frustration and surprise. The entire assembly remained in hushed silence and Jyestha reveled in their terror.

"Then, I demand your crown, the one upon your head."

Chaos erupted over her words. The Asuras screamed and fought, in utter panic. Voices were raised in dissent. Virochana, grim and stone faced raised his hands to his head and took off the crown that was the crux of his invincibility. He placed it in front of her. Jyestha received the crown and placed it on her own head.

"You are not Lakshmi." Virochana whispered at the gesture. Jyestha smirked. The play was nearing its finale, and she should break it to him now.

"No. I am Alakshmi, the goddess of misfortune."

Jyestha vanished from the assembly, with the crown and Virochana's doom resounded in the form of her loud scornful laughter that made the Asuras cover their ears. Soon, as the real Lakshmi manifested in Vaikuntha, Lord Vishnu slayed Virochana and the other asuras in a fierce battle with the help of the Devas who had recovered their strength.

For Jyestha, it was the sweetest victory, however it was far from the end.

10.

Jyestha Devi

Vaikuntha. Jyestha stood transfixed by the waters of the Kshirsagara. She touched the waters of the ocean of milk, as though she were saluting her mother. Jyestha's eyes were filled with tears.

"*Priye*, do not weep." Kali was at her side. Jyestha's heart was full of conflicting emotions. The pair had been unable to believe it when the summons came from Vaikuntha, requesting their presence in the assembly conducted on Mount Meru. They had almost declined the invitation. In the aftermath of the battle Kali and Jyestha agreed that they would never set foot in Devaloka again. They would content themselves with *Mrityuloka* or Patala or build a hut on the banks of the river Pushpabhadra and renounce the world.

"Why are we being summoned? I do not wish to stand in judgement in front of the Trimurti and the Devas." Jyestha murmured. Anxiety ate at her heart and not even Kali's logical reasons assuaged her fears. When the infamous pair entered the assembly of the gods, a hush fell among the audience. Jyestha and Kali stood uncomfortably, casting fearful glances at their jury. The assembly was overcrowded. Brahma, Vishnu and Shiva held the highest seats.

Jyestha bowed to her lord, Mahadeva before paying her respects to everyone else. When the assembly was silent Lord Brahma began to speak.

"We are gathered here to witness the trial of Alakshmi. Alakshmi, the goddess of misfortune was born from the churning of the ocean with her twin, Lakshmi. While their fortunes were opposite, the sister pair worked for the benefit of the Devas, due to which Virochana was slain. Devi, we may have some grievances to address."

When the Devas bowed to heads in respect, Jyestha felt painfully embarrassed. It was only when Kali nudged her to keep her head held high, that she straightened and accepted their gesture with humility. Jyestha's eyes darted to Lakshmi, who stood in the wing reserved for the female goddesses. Lakshmi was smiling.

Lord Shiva began by recounting Jyestha's history which made her want to vanish again. The Lord reciting her list of positive and negative deeds made her feel like a criminal, it would be the Lord she worshiped who would pass the judgement on Jyestha and Kali. Kali retained his composure. He listened his list of offence with an unbothered air.

"Do either of you have anything to say in your defense?"

Jyestha and Kali shook their heads.

"We would say we deserve any punishment that you decide. Our schemes put the three worlds in immense danger, and we nearly destroyed the order of the universe."

Lord Shiva smiled. The same benevolent smile that he had bestowed on Jyestha when she had appeared from the churning of the ocean.

"It appears they repent their actions. However, we cannot ignore that Jyestha Devi's brilliant thinking put an end to Virochana's tyranny. What she has done is incomparable and an act of true selflessness, where she valued the lives that populate this universe over her personal vendetta. That is true *karuna*."

Jyestha stared, thunderstruck by the verdict.

"In truth, it is Jyestha Devi who has been wronged." Jyestha startled at the voice of Lord Vishnu who spoke out of turn.

"The churning of the ocean birthed Jyestha and Lakshmi who are two sides of the same divinity. While Lakshmi is the gentle and benevolent aspect of *Prakriti*, Jyestha is the fearsome and protective aspect of the same goddess. Her energies were channeled wrongly due to the negative connotation assigned to her. Instead of respect, she was feared, and it was this fear and rejection that caused discord in the three worlds. While Jyestha's role is to cause discord and she furthers the narrative of the cosmos in her own way, the essence of the lotus does not change even if its colours are different."

So, I am not inauspicious? Why do I still feel guilty?

"Jyestha Devi, to amend the error of the gods, you shall be worshiped. The householders that worship the gods shall assign a portion to you before making any offerings to Lakshmi. The Asvattha tree shall remain your place of worship and your symbols will be the blue lotus, the broom and the kamandalu. You are no longer '*Alakshmi*' the goddess of misfortune, but Jyestha, the sister of Lakshmi who guards her devotees from misfortune." Lord Shiva's utterance reverberated in the assembly hall. Hearing the auspicious sounds, Jyestha bowed her head in reverence.

"However, neither you nor Kali can stay in Devaloka, you shall not have a permanent abode but wander in the three worlds as per your preference. Is there anything you wish to say?"

Jyestha glanced at her husband and ventured.

"Can Kali keep his post of the Yuga Purusha? It would be beneficial to the gods in the future."

"We won't remove him from his post, however, Kali cannot be allowed to interfere in the working of the Devas." The jury ended. Kali and Jyestha left Vaikuntha. Jyestha would have liked to meet Lakshmi, but it would be an awkward meeting. They had a complicated history. Jyestha still needed time to sort out her emotions about the proceedings and the newfound emotions towards her family.

"You are not angry that we shall have to wander from place to place?" Kali asked as they traversed the silvery sands on the banks of the Sarasvati in Devaloka. Jyestha wanted to visit Dussaha's hermitage to refresh her memories. Jyestha paused as she filled her kamandalu with the water from the sacred river.

"I am used to wandering, my lord. Perhaps it is you who shall become fidgety since you will not have any *apasaras* to charm." Jyestha quipped. Her lord husband groaned at her sarcasm.

"I can always charm you." Kali murmured. He casually plucked the blue lotus that bloomed on the banks and handed it to her. Kali's face was tinged with remorse.

"I am sorry for how I acted when I became a king, and for spreading all those rumours. I do not know what had gotten into me. I felt as though I was letting you down. Jyestha, I am not a decent Gandharva. I became blinded by pride and arrogance, and I failed to listen to you. Are you sure you wish to stay by my side?"

Jyestha clutched the blue lotus in her palm. Did he expect her to leave after he had so vehemently declared his love for her? The Gandharvas were lovers of beautiful women, however Jyestha had never been a great beauty. Yet Kali had chosen her.

"My lord, I stay by your side because I see myself in you. We have the same insecurities, and we understand each other. My first marriage was not a great source of happiness because Dussaha never understood me. But with you, I can be content." Jyestha raised her eyes to gaze directly at her husband and smiled charmingly.

With Kali I can be content. That is what was lacking in my life all along. The sense of contentment that I feel with him cannot be matched by any opulence in the universe.

"Thank you, priye."

The scent of the blue lotus wafted along Jyestha's nose. This was the fragrance she had chased along the banks of the Sarasvati but had never been able to identify it. Jyestha sought herself. She found her identity in the end.

I am Jyestha, the elder. The Goddess of Discord.

Epilogue

On the eve of Deepavali, Jyestha wandered in disguise among the humans in Mrityuloka. Due to the rules of her worship set up by the Trimurti, Jyestha gained many devotees. She would bless their homes from afar so that no misfortune touched it.

The Asvattha tree in Vishashan became an important landmark in the worship of the Devi. Thousands of lamps were lit at its circumference during the festivities. Women prayed for the blessings of Jyestha and offered her favorite peppered khichadi with a squeeze of lime. Sour lemons and chilies were kept as a symbol of protection from the goddess.

Sometimes, Jyestha and Lakshmi's paths crossed. When they did, they engaged in a friendly match of dice to remember the old times and laughed over the ongoing drama in the realms of the Devas, Asuras and the humans. Jyestha and Kali essayed their negative roles in this stage-play, and they still do take the centre stage in Kali Yuga. As Jyestha Devi once said:

If this Brahmanda is an ongoing stage-play, then it deserves a befitting villain.

However, at the end of the day, Lakshmi and Jyestha are family. The two sisters are two faces of the feminine that essay a different role. It is their dynamism that keeps this play running.

Aboli Mane is an author and blogger born in Goa; raised in Mumbai. Aboli has a strong affinity for writing in fantasy, mythology, and paranormal genres. She enjoys writing short stories due to her deep love of creating new characters and concepts.

A published poet, she published her debut poetry book *"An Aster's Solitude"* in 2019. Her poems were included in various anthologies like *"Foraging"* by Globalage Poetry and *"Secrets"* by the Write Order.

In 2023, her paranormal short story *"The Shiroyama Ritual"* was published in the anthology *"The Selection of a Sacred Strawberry"* among the winning short stories of the international premier league short-story contest *"PenFluenza 3.0"*, organized by WriteFluence. Her story was featured among 28 literary works.

In 2023, her romantic short story *"Sunflowers in Rain"* was shortlisted in *Ruskin Bond's #WriteForLove Contest* organised by

Mugafi and is listed among 20 winning stories and she enlisted in their *Author Fellowship Program* to further her writing career and publish her current novel.

You can reach out to her on Instagram at *@aboli_poetry* or visit her blog *A Writer in the Room.*

We love creating beautiful books for you!

Be a part of our ever-growing community of authors.
Grow, write, and publish with us!

Connect with us on socials.
We'd love to hear from you!

@InkfeathersPublishing

www.ingramcontent.com/pod-product-compliance
Lightning Source LLC
LaVergne TN
LVHW090131160826
845673LV00017B/2112

* 9 7 8 8 1 1 9 4 8 3 6 6 2 *